Praise for
Michele Bardsley

Cupid, Inc.

"WOW . . . this is an erotic romance that truly hits the mark. There are great, detailed scenes that leave you panting for more."
—The Romance Readers Connection

"A top-notch quartet of tales that are guaranteed to singe your fingers. . . . What an enjoyable way to get revved up for Valentine's Day by spending it reading *Cupid, Inc.*"
—Romance Reviews Today

"I love Michele Bardsley's *Cupid, Inc.*! It's sexy and erotic and the humor will make you grin at the same time you're squirming in your seat."   —Cheyenne McCray, author of *Forbidden Magic*

"Her understanding of people's need to love and be loved is uncanny, and it is no small wonder that *Cupid, Inc.* is such a wonderful read. . . . Michele Bardsley has a wonderful knack for writing a page-turner that is not only enjoyable but also witty and full of good humor . . . a wonderful book!"
—Roundtable Reviews

"I enjoyed each and every one of these stories. I love stories with the gods and goddesses in them and this collection is one of the best!"   —The Best Reviews

"A wonderful anthology about four couples and their fantasies . . . one great read!"   —Fallen Angel Reviews

"The concept is cute and the personalities of the deities are entertaining."   —*Romantic Times*

continued . . .

I'm the Vampire, That's Why

"From the first sentence, Michele grabbed me and didn't let me go! A vampire mom? PTA meetings? A sulky teenager? Throw in a gorgeous, ridiculously hot hero and you've got the paranormal romance of the year. Get this one *now*."   —MaryJanice Davidson

"Hot, hilarious, one helluva ride. . . . Michele Bardsley weaves a sexily delicious tale spun from the heart."   —L. A. Banks

"A fun, fun read!"   —Rosemary Laurey

"Michele Bardsley has penned the funniest, quirkiest, coolest vampire tale you'll ever read. It's hot and funny and sad and wonderful, the kind of story you can't put down and won't forget. Definitely one for the keeper shelf."   —Kate Douglas

"An amusing vampire romance . . . a terrific contemporary tale."
—The Best Reviews

"Written with a dash of humor reminiscent of Katie MacAlister . . . amusing."   —Monsters and Critics

"A marvelous introduction to the world of vampires and werewolves . . . funny and filled with explosive sexual tension."
—The Romance Readers Connection

"Add the name Michele Bardsley to the ranks of talented paranormal authors who wield humor as a deft weapon. . . . Both the characters and the world scenario offer loads of possibilities for further adventures, which means there are many more hours of reading pleasure ahead!"   —*Romantic Times*

Fantasyland

· ·

Michele Bardsley

A SIGNET ECLIPSE BOOK

SIGNET ECLIPSE
Published by New American Library, a division of
Penguin Group (USA) Inc., 375 Hudson Street,
New York, New York 10014, USA
Penguin Group (Canada), 90 Eglinton Avenue East, Suite 700, Toronto,
Ontario M4P 2Y3, Canada (a division of Pearson Penguin Canada Inc.)
Penguin Books Ltd., 80 Strand, London WC2R 0RL, England
Penguin Ireland, 25 St. Stephen's Green, Dublin 2,
Ireland (a division of Penguin Books Ltd.)
Penguin Group (Australia), 250 Camberwell Road, Camberwell, Victoria 3124,
Australia (a division of Pearson Australia Group Pty. Ltd.)
Penguin Books India Pvt. Ltd., 11 Community Centre, Panchsheel Park,
New Delhi - 110 017, India
Penguin Group (NZ), 67 Apollo Drive, Rosedale, North Shore 0632,
New Zealand (a division of Pearson New Zealand Ltd.)
Penguin Books (South Africa) (Pty.) Ltd., 24 Sturdee Avenue,
Rosebank, Johannesburg 2196, South Africa

Penguin Books Ltd., Registered Offices:
80 Strand, London WC2R 0RL, England

First published by Signet Eclipse, an imprint of New American Library,
a division of Penguin Group (USA) Inc.

First Printing, November 2007
10 9 8 7 6 5 4 3 2 1

LIBRARY OF CONGRESS CATALOGING-IN-PUBLICATION DATA:
Bardsley, Michele.
    Fantasyland/by Michele Bardsley.
        p. cm.
    ISBN: 978-0-451-22223-7
    I. Title.

PS3602.A7753F36   2007
813'.6—dc22   2007018006

Set in Goudy Old Style
Designed by Ginger Legato

Printed in the United States of America

To my sister Julii and her husband, Ryan

Contents

Fantasyland

Fantasyland

Dear Adventurer,

Thank you for requesting information about Fantasyland Resort. Inside this package you will find brochures about our themed islands, a DVD that gives you a visual tour of our facilities, our preapplication, and the price list of our packaged deals. You can also create a custom vacation by choosing from our menu of à la carte services.

Almost nothing is forbidden on our island retreats, but we do insist that you adhere to a few important rules, which include:

1. Guests must be twenty-one or older to play at our resort.
2. All physical contact between resort guests and/or staff members must be consensual.
3. Guests of the resort must follow the posted guidelines in our play areas to ensure the safety and comfort of all participants.

Fantasyland's islands are privately owned and under no governmental jurisdiction. We take your safety, your pleasure, and your comfort very seriously at Fantasy-land, which is why we employ Safety Agents. Each SA is well trained in the martial arts and has extensive knowledge and experience in the security field. Guests are expected to adhere to the requests of our Safety Agents.

Our application process ensures that guests meet the mental and physical requirements necessary to enjoy a vacation at our resort. Any application missing medical or financial data will be denied. Once your paperwork is approved, we will accept your deposit and assign your Personal Vacation Planner.

Your PVP will help you create the perfect fantasy vacation based on your needs and your budget. Be assured that you will experience the ultimate in pampering and pleasure, no matter which island or package you choose.

We look forward to hearing from you soon.

Sincerely,
Julia P. Edgemont
Director, Fantasyland Resort

Two to One

Île de Plaisir

On Île de Plaisir, guests will find "the more, the merrier" an apt phrase. Guests who enjoy multiplicity in all their activities will find our exclusive little island the perfect, safe port to indulge the wildest of fantasies.

Our restaurants, hotels, dance clubs, and play areas cater to plenitude. Whether you participate in polyamorous relationships or you simply want to try the sensual thrills of multipartner hookups, Île de Plaisir will offer you numerous sensual opportunities.

There is no better name for our island than "pleasure" since that is all you will experience. Because good things always come in threes . . . or more.

One
·······

"This whole place is beautiful," said Carrie Tremont as she entered the hotel suite. Her husband, Greg, followed her, hauling their bags inside. The hotel had been crowded and busy, so they'd decided not to wait around for a bellboy.

So far, Greg hadn't revealed much about his anniversary surprise. They'd been married ten years. Their five-year-old twins were at Disney World with their grandparents. As much as she missed her boys, she also missed her husband. They rarely got uninterrupted time alone.

Carrie tossed her purse on the couch. Wow. The living room looked both luxurious and comfortable. The decor was modern; everything from the furniture to the paintings was straight, clean lines. The colors weren't typical hotel browns and crèmes, either. The couch was red, the table black, and the floor lamps gold.

The open kitchenette was located behind the living room, all stark black, even the appliances. On the counter, she saw the bottle of champagne in a gleaming gold bucket, along with two flutes. Nice.

Past the tiny kitchen was a pair of French doors that opened onto a large balcony. On the left was the door to the bedroom. She went inside and saw the same color scheme. The bed, which was black from its frame to its plush pillows, wasn't exactly typical, either. It was huge.

"How many people do they expect to sleep in that bed?" she asked as Greg dragged their suitcases into the room. She laughed. "We could fit a small car in it!"

Greg put down their bags. Her darling nerd blinked at her behind his horn-rimmed glasses. "I think you'll find lots of stuff here is very interesting."

Her stomach squeezed in anticipation. What had he planned? Had he . . . ? No, he'd never go for *that*.

"We still have three hours until our dinner reservation," he said. "We could go to the pool or take a walk on the beach."

"I have an idea about how to spend the time." She took his hand and led him to the huge bed. "Stay here."

She hurried into the bathroom. She took off her pants, blouse, hose, and shoes. She'd worn the new bra and panties she'd purchased at Victoria's Secret.

Fantasyland

She looked herself over. No point to freshen her makeup. She fluffed out her short blond hair. For a thirty-three-year-old woman who'd borne twins, she didn't look half bad.

Good thing she'd indulged in a spa day prior to their trip. She had had facial treatments, a mani-pedi, and leg and bikini waxes. She pulled her panties down and looked at her bare pussy. She usually got a wax that left a strip of hair. Greg would be really surprised to see her completely bare.

Early in their relationship, Carrie had asked Greg about his sexual fantasies. His reply: "You, naked."

That really did seem to be the extent of what he wanted. Maybe Greg's sexual needs weren't complex.

And that was why she feared talking to him about *her* needs. What she desired was a tad more complicated than "You, naked."

Not that it mattered. Most of the time, they fell into bed at night too exhausted to make love. Sex wasn't as exciting as it had been in the early days.

Their lack of physical intimacy bled into other areas. She didn't feel as close to him as she had pre-twins. Her married friends told her that was the nature of marriage, especially after parenthood. Sex was shoved to the bottom of the priority list.

And yet Carrie found herself fantasizing about getting thoroughly ravished by two men.

Last month, she had sat at her kitchen table with her sister. They drank iced tea and chatted. Carrie told her older sis about her fantasy. Shelley had teased her about such naughty thoughts, and Carrie had dropped the subject. It wasn't something she could talk to Greg about. He would never share her with another man. And it wasn't like she wanted two husbands or even a husband and a boyfriend. She loved Greg and their life together.

She just wanted her sex life back, damn it.

Somewhere along the way, she realized that denying her sexual desires, no matter how strange they might appear to others, was wrong. She needed to tell Greg her fantasies—even if they couldn't really have a second man in their bed.

"Baby? Are you okay?" Greg knocked on the bathroom door and jolted her out of her thoughts.

Carrie straightened. "Be out in a sec."

When she reentered the bedroom, she found Greg sprawled naked on the bed. His gaze caressed her body in a way that had heat pulsing through her.

She crawled onto the bed and into his arms. For a long moment, Greg just stared at her.

"You're gorgeous." His lips captured hers. She melted into his arms and deepened their contact. Yum. He tasted like those peppermint Tic Tacs he loved to chew on all the time.

Desire and need streaked through her, pooling wet and hot between her thighs. Reaching between them, she stroked his cock.

Greg's hands tangled in her hair as he deepened the kiss, thrusting his tongue inside to mate with hers. Then his lips moved down her throat, his tongue flicking the dimple at its base. Carrie moaned as he nuzzled the skin between her breasts, raining kisses over the flesh exposed by her push-up bra.

He reached around and unhooked her bra. After tossing it to the floor, he cupped her breasts in his hands and squeezed. Oh, he felt so good. And for once she didn't have to worry about the twins interrupting their lovemaking.

His mouth closed over one turgid nipple. Sensations rippled through her. He suckled her other nipple, giving it the same torturous attention.

"Greg," she sighed, her hands threading through his silky hair, "that feels so good, honey."

His hand coasted down her stomach and slid into her panties.

"What the—" His desire-glazed eyes found hers. She smiled as his fingers stroked her bare flesh. "Mmm. I want to see you."

He crawled between her legs and dragged her underwear off. He stared at her naked pussy. "That is a beautiful sight."

"You like?"

"I love." He settled down and pressed his mouth against her vulva. "You've never done anything like this before."

"I'm trying new things."

"Thank God." He kissed her again. His tongue wiggled down her slit.

Her pussy was already hot and wet and ready. He licked

the evidence of her desire off her inner thighs, then dove inside her entrance.

Carrie gasped as pleasure ricocheted through her. Greg's tongue darted in and out of her, the strokes rough and fast.

Her hips pumped to match his rhythm. Her hands fisted in the bedspread as she felt bliss coil tight and hot. Then his mouth moved to her clit and closed over it, sucking hard. Just as an orgasm threatened to overwhelm her, he stopped.

"Greg!"

He chuckled.

An ache settled between her thighs. Her pussy pulsed in need, in want.

Greg once again suckled her clit. Then he inserted two fingers into her pussy. The thrust of his fingers matched the thrusts of his tongue.

The orgasm built, higher and higher. Just as she would've tipped over the edge, Greg stopped again.

"I swear to God I'm going to kill you," she muttered.

He kissed each of her hips and licked her belly. His lips found every inch of skin between her pussy and her breasts. He felt so good. She'd missed being with him like this. How wonderful to feel him touch her, kiss her. Love threaded through her desire.

He moved on top of her, parted her thighs, and entered her in one swift stroke. Carrie gasped. God, *that* felt fantastic! She wrapped her legs around his waist and surged forward, meeting his every thrust.

With one hand, he captured her wrists and raised her arms above her head. His cock filled her; his motions were slow, steady, and tender.

Waves of pleasure crested through her. Oh, yes!

He released her wrists, looped his arms under her shoulders, and pounded into her. He groaned—the sound caught against her flesh. He was as lost as she in the moment. She bucked against him, her clit throbbing.

"Carrie," he panted. "Oh, honey, you feel so good."

The denied orgasm quivered for an endless moment . . . then burst. She was carried away by the intensity of it. She clutched Greg as she rode the wave.

It took her a little while to realize that Greg had stopped moving. She blinked up at him. "You didn't come."

"We're trying new things, remember?"

"Your new thing is not to come?" she asked doubtfully.

He grinned. "I want to . . ." He hesitated. Then he said, "I want to fuck your breasts."

Two
. . . .

C arrie's pulse jumped. Who was this man? And what had he done with her husband? They'd never tried breast fucking before.

"Do you want to try it?" Greg asked.

She looked at him, her lips hitching into a naughty grin, and she squeezed her breasts together. So far, their tenth-anniversary celebration was turning out better than she had ever dreamed.

He unsheathed his cock from her cunt, then scooted forward until his knees were even with her arms. He slid his cock into the tight space created by her pushed-together breasts. He braced his hands against the wall.

The intimacy of having his cock so close to her face was a little unnerving. His penis was so wet from her come that it was lubricated enough to slide against her skin. He started moving slow, but soon increased his pace, groaning and panting. Wow. He liked it.

"Carrie," he managed through clenched teeth, "let me come in your mouth."

She wasn't opposed to swallowing his semen, but it wasn't something she often did, either. She was excited about making him go over the edge, about doing wicked things with the man she loved.

He stopped thrusting and pushed the tip of his cock against her lips. Precome pearled there and she licked the salty drop.

"Take me, Carrie."

She opened her mouth, and allowed him to slide between her lips. She cupped his balls with one hand and curled the other around the base of his cock. She suckled his head while her hands stroked the hard flesh of his penis and the round softness of his balls.

"Yes!" he cried.

He pushed his cock farther into her mouth and she clamped her lips around it. He jerked once, twice—hot come spewed into her mouth. She swallowed it with surprising ease, drinking from him until his cock stopped trembling.

Greg eased away from her mouth and flopped onto the bed.

"Wow," he said.

"Yeah," said Carrie. "Wow."

* * *

They dozed together. Carrie was the first to stir. She kissed Greg's jaw, dragging her lips down his neck, then back up again. Her fingers curled around his cock and stroked.

Her computer nerd sure was built. Brown hair lightly furred his pectorals and stomach. Because he spent hours sitting at a desk working on computers, he countered the lack of movement by running three or four miles every night.

With lips and tongue, Carrie worked her way to his pectorals, detouring to one coin-sized areola and its tiny, hard peak. She tugged it between her teeth, flicking the tip.

His eyes fluttered open.

She moved farther down his chest, exploring the muscled ridges of his stomach with hands and mouth.

Slipping between his legs, she grasped his shaft and caressed it. His cock hardened under her ministrations. Cupping his balls, she licked and sucked his mushroom head.

"Carrie!" His thighs tensed.

Her heart revved into overdrive as lust thickened. The musky scent of his sex excited her. She went down on him all the way, sucking his manhood as she fondled his sac.

Then she released his cock and sat up.

He looked at her, his expression pained.

She scooted up, pressing her knees on either side of his hips and guided his swollen member into her pussy.

Greg cupped her breasts, gently twisting her nipples.

Pleasure roared through her.

"Yeah, honey. Hmm. I love that, Greg."

Sensations raced from her breasts to her pussy. Greg continued to play with her breasts as she moved back and forth, working his cock in and out of her pussy.

Carrie pressed her palms against his chest, and for a moment, she thought about what it would be like to have another man behind her, his cock plunging into her ass while Greg fucked her pussy.

The very idea of having two men seated fully inside her sent the first tingles of an orgasm rippling through her.

Greg released her breasts and grabbed her hips. He pounded into her. His eyes were glazed, his face tight as he thrust toward his own completion.

He's fucking me, too. You're watching him and me and it's such a turn-on. For all of us.

Her bliss erupted and her cunt convulsed so hard, his cock slipped out. She rubbed her pussy over and over on his shaft. All the while she thought about the mystery man who would plow her rear, and she felt the rise of another orgasm. God! Yes!

"I'm coming!" Greg's groan intertwined with her low cries, and then he was ejaculating, his come spurting onto his stomach. She went over the edge again, her whole body aflame as she rode a second wave into bliss.

When she opened her eyes, she found Greg studying her face.

"Why do you close your eyes?" he asked. "What do you think about?"

"I think about the way you make me feel." Guilt stabbed her because she knew that wasn't the right answer. Greg was very intuitive. He knew something was up. But he was also patient. He would wait for her to reveal her secrets.

She rolled off onto the bed and took his hand in hers. "I love you."

"I love you, too." He looked at the digital clock on the nightstand. "We'd better take showers and get going. Dinner's in an hour."

In the bathroom, Carrie finished layering on her mascara. After putting on her red lipstick, she considered herself critically in the mirror.

Her blond hair was worn in a page cut that highlighted her angular face. She had decent cheekbones and cornflower blue eyes, but she'd always felt her lips were too thin and her forehead a touch too wide. Her bangs dealt with that imperfection.

She considered the rest of the package. A few inches over five feet, she had decent legs and a nice rack, if she did say so herself. Her red dress was strapless and stopped midthigh. She didn't need a bra with it since the top had built-in support.

Her high heels had straps that tied around the ankles. They gave her three more inches, too.

The only jewelry she wore was the diamond stud earrings Greg had given her for Christmas and her princess-cut diamond wedding ring.

"You look beautiful," Greg said.

Smiling, Claire turned to her husband, who lounged in the doorway. Greg had once described himself as unremarkable, but she found him adorable. The facial features he called average, she thought of as handsome. The brown eyes he called dishwater dull sparkled like amber to her. His dark hair was naturally curly, so he kept it short, but not too short. She loved running her fingers through it.

He'd opted for contacts, but she thought his glasses made him look really cute. She loved her gorgeous nerd. He wore a nice white dress shirt tucked into a pair of black dress pants. His shoes were also black and shiny. His jacket was draped over his arm.

"Are you ready, honey?"

"Yes," she said. "Let's go."

"I thought we were going to dinner," said Carrie. They'd taken the elevator to the top floor. She had expected some kind of expensive restaurant, but instead, the doors opened into a very luxurious penthouse suite.

They stood in the marble foyer. Greg held her hand tightly and made no move to venture farther into the space. Was it just her or did he seem nervous?

"Good evening, Mr. and Mrs. Tremont."

Carrie turned to greet the clone of Brad Pitt. She stared at him, dumbfounded. He was gorgeous—the kind of gorgeous that belonged on a movie screen. He wore his blond hair short and spiked. His eyes were a brilliant green. But he had the square jaw and chiseled good looks of GQ models and soap opera stars. He was dressed in a tuxedo that fit his broad shoulders very well.

He shook hands with Greg. Then he reached out and took Carrie's hand, which he kissed. "I'm Marc."

"And you're a waiter?" asked Carrie, confused.

He flashed a devastating grin. "No, Mrs. Tremont. I'm your anniversary present."

Three
· · · · · · · · ·

Carrie looked at her husband. "You're giving me a waiter?"

Greg smiled, but his eyes seemed filled with doubt. "I'm giving you a threesome."

Carrie's mouth dropped open. She turned a wide gaze to her husband. Her heart skipped a beat.

"I'll go check on the champagne," said Marc. "Join me in the living room when you're ready."

He left them alone, but Carrie barely noticed. Her knees had gone watery. "You're giving me *what*?"

"I overheard your conversation with Shelley. I know our sex life isn't all that exciting. It's been stressful for you. You gave up your career to stay home with the boys. My hours are crazy and I have to travel all the time. God, Carrie, I love you so much, I want to give you the world."

25

"I have you and the boys," she said softly. "That's what is important to me."

"I know." He looked at her, his brown eyes shining with passion. "Let me make your fantasy come true."

"Are you sure?" she asked. Her belly warbled in anticipation. "Because I would never jeopardize what we have together for some sexual exploit. I can live without a threesome, but I can't live without you."

Greg cupped her face and looked her in the eyes. "I want this for you, for us." He kissed her. "Happy anniversary, honey."

Carrie was too nervous to eat, though there was a sumptuous spread laid out in the dining room. Her hunger was building, but it wasn't the kind of hunger that would be assuaged by paté and caviar.

Marc was definitely a roll-with-the-punches kind of guy. He merely pointed her into the bedroom with its four-poster bed and asked her to get undressed.

Greg stayed in the living room.

"Lie on the bed and close your eyes," said Marc.

"I've never done anything like this. Neither has Greg."

"He wants to give you pleasure, Carrie. We both do. But first we have to see how compatible we are. Greg knows the procedures. It was all outlined when he bought the package."

"Okay." Carrie took off her clothes and high heels. She still couldn't believe Greg had hired a man to help him fuck his wife. Love mixed with excitement, with doubt. Would he regret sharing her? Or would this be an once-in-a-life-time experience that brought them closer together?

She crawled into the huge bed and settled against the pillows. Giddy with the prospect of what was about to un-fold, she lay on her bed naked, and luxuriated in the soft sheets.

She closed her eyes.

Marc wasted no time—she'd give him that. After a few moments, during which she heard the whispers of discarded clothing, she felt the bed dip under his weight.

He straddled her and her eyes flew open. Her heart pounded erratically. He was Adonis personified: muscled, tanned, hairless. Did he wax? *Focus, Carrie.* Holy God! His cock was huge and the damned thing wasn't even hard yet.

It all felt so surreal.

"Close your eyes, Carrie."

Her eyes fluttered closed again.

His hands stroked her breasts, cupping and molding. Her nipples puckered, aching to be touched, to be kissed. He circled one finger around her areola, teasing her nipples with the brush of his fingertips.

"I want to taste you," he whispered. "Is that okay?"

"Please."

Her nipples were hard, aching points. His lips closed over one taut peak. He suckled, his tongue swirling against the sensitive flesh.

A low moan rose from her throat as hot desire speared her. He cupped her other breast and used his tongue to torment it. Moisture seeped from her pussy, which pulsed in invitation.

"I don't know about you," she managed. "But I think we have heat."

"Me, too." He scooted lower. His lips pressed against her quivering stomach muscles and his tongue traced an invisible line to her navel.

Carrie felt submerged in desire. Her pussy convulsed, trembled. Marc's hands coasted to her hips, his mouth nibbling to the edge of her pussy. He was so close to her clit.

His tongue wiggled down her slit, and his soft lips dragged sensually across her swelling flesh. He encircled her entrance, teasing her ruthlessly. Then, to her shock, he licked the bit of flesh between her anus and vagina.

Her breathing went erratic and her body went hot and tingly.

He grabbed her buttocks and pushed her legs up. Then he pressed his mouth against her clit. His hot breath ghosted over the sensitive nub.

Carrie shuddered.

His tongue began stroking her clit in a rhythm that drove her wild. Just as she felt the rise of an orgasm, the bastard stopped.

Once again, her eyes flew open. What the hell was it with men and their bad timing? Sheesh!

She swallowed her protests. Here she was with another man, enjoying his lovemaking. Guilt assailed her, even though Greg had given her this gift.

"Relax," he murmured. "Your husband will join us soon."

Did the man read minds, too? No. He was probably just used to comforting nervous housewives.

Marc rose to his knees. One finger slid over her clit, offering her both relief and agitation. God, she wanted to come.

"Hold on to your ankles," said Marc, pushing her legs up farther.

She wrapped her hands around her ankles and offered him even greater access to her cunt.

As his finger slowly stroked her clitoris, he formed a beak with the fingers of his other hand. To her amazement, he slowly pushed them into her pussy.

She sucked in deep breaths. The pressure was intense and the feeling was . . . God! She couldn't even think of a word to describe how it felt for his entire hand to surge inside her.

"Relax," he said again. "This is for your pleasure. Enjoy it."

Carrie made a conscious effort to loosen up. She untensed her body, though her grip on her ankles remained a little too firm.

When he'd filled her up to his wrist, stretching her vaginal walls, he curled his fingers into a fist.

Carrie moaned. His fist lodged in her pussy felt so strange—and yet so good. Then . . . oh then . . . his knuckles began to rhythmically bump on the underside of her entrance, tapping against her G-spot.

The fondling of her clit and the manipulation of her pussy's most erotic spot tossed her into blinding pleasure.

The intensity of the orgasm tore a scream from her throat.

She was awash in the light and heat of absolute bliss. As the last waves of her orgasm rippled through her, Marc removed his hand and sat back.

"God." Carrie sucked in a steadying breath. "That was . . . unbelievable."

"Thank you. But there's more in store for you, sweet Carrie. It's time for your husband to come in. Are you ready?"

"Yes," said Carrie. She wasn't sure if she was ready for two men, but she was damned sure gonna give it a try.

Four
· · · · · · · ·

When Greg entered the room, Marc pulled Carrie onto his lap and held her by the waist.

She felt instantly guilty—as if she were an adulterer about to be caught by her husband.

"Take a deep breath," he murmured.

She sucked in a deep breath and blew it out.

As Greg got undressed, his gaze carefully blank, Marc cupped her breasts and played with her nipples. She sat across his thighs, his hard cock nestled against her crotch. He twitched it against her pussy, causing trembles of need. Oh, God.

Greg stood on the side of the bed, looking at them.

"Join us, Greg," said Marc. "Let's make love to your wife."

Carrie felt the blood rush out of her face. Greg looked as

though he regretted this whole fantasy idea. She wanted to smooth away the furrows on his brow, talk to him until the pain left his eyes.

His cock was soft, but she hoped that wouldn't be the case for long. Marc leaned forward, cupped her neck, and brought his lips to her ear.

"He loves you so much." The tip of his tongue traced the shell of her ear. "What do you want to do?"

She wanted to show Greg how much she loved him. How much she needed him.

He climbed on the bed, casting an unsure look at Marc. "What do we do?"

Carrie crawled off Marc and into Greg's arms. "I want you," she whispered. She cupped his face and stared into his amber eyes. "Thank you. But if you don't want to go through with it—"

"I want to," he reassured her. He seemed to relax a little. "Your pleasure is my pleasure."

Carrie caressed the hard cocks and tense balls of the two men on either side of her. Marc and Greg pleasured her breasts, their hot mouths and slick tongues tormenting her nipples.

Once again, the heat of desire engulfed her. Greg tugged her nipple between his teeth, and she gasped at the sharp pleasure.

"Greg. Marc."

They lifted their heads and looked at her; both of their

gazes were dark with need. Her pulse jumped, and she licked her lips. They were both so damned gorgeous.

Greg's hand coasted across her stomach, leaving streaks of tickly heat in his path.

"Remember what we did in the hotel room, Greg? With my breasts?"

"Hell, yes."

Her grin was wicked. "Let's do it again." She looked at Marc and fluttered her eyelashes outrageously. "My pussy will need attention."

Marc scooted between her legs, and waited to see what Greg would do. Her husband found the lubricant and squirted some between her breasts.

Carrie squeezed her breasts together. Greg straddled her, leaning forward to hold on to the bed's headboard, and pushed his hard cock between her soft mounds of flesh. She loved it when Greg played with her breasts and nipples. It was as if an electric wire connected her nipples to her pussy.

Carrie pinched her nipples, gasping at the erotic zaps, and watched her husband's cock fuck her breasts.

He pumped faster, his grunts and groans increasing with his pace. He really was a breast man.

Marc suckled her clit.

Carrie pushed her breasts closer to tighten the gap, and twisted her nipples faster and harder. Marc worked her clit hard, licking and sucking. Pleasure rose quickly, almost too quickly, and burst.

Her pussy throbbed with exquisite release.

"Carrie!" Greg's hot seed spurted onto her neck, his cock trembling between her sweat-slickened breasts.

She released her breasts and leaned forward to lick Greg's cock. He shifted positions so she could take more of his shaft into her mouth. She licked off his musky essence.

"Hmm," said Carrie. "What's next?"

Marc grinned. "We're going to make your fantasy come true."

Greg kissed her, a slow meeting of the lips that made Carrie's heart pound. She sighed into his mouth, suckling his bottom lip, tracing the upper one before spearing the seam. He tasted like peppermint Tic Tacs. He groaned and she swallowed the sound, angling her head to taste more of him. His tongue danced with hers.

As Greg released her mouth and kissed her jaw, Marc's hand coasted down her back. Desire speared her. Oh, God. Two men making love to her. She could barely wrap her brain around it.

"Lay down between us," said Marc.

Carrie lay on her back. Marc was on her left and Greg was on her right. Marc seemed content to watch her and Greg. Her husband had apparently gotten over his doubts. Or maybe the idea of another man sharing their bed, sharing her, turned him on, too.

His mouth traveled along her collarbone and down the

valley between her breasts. His tongue traced one areola; then he tasted her nipple. He licked and laved. She pressed his head against her chest and moaned.

Marc leaned down and kissed her. Carrie felt a jolt of electricity.

Greg's groan shuddered across her flesh as his lips clamped the nipple and suckled it into a taut, aching peak. His other hand cupped her left breast, kneading it, two fingers pinching its hardening point.

Marc's kiss deepened. Carrie didn't know what to do with herself. Her body hummed in anticipation.

"I want your cocks in my mouth," she said. "Please!"

Both men rolled onto their backsides. She scooted between them and looked at the male buffet before her. Greg's eyes were glazed, his body trembling, and his cock hardening. Marc's cock was still hard from their previous play. She grasped both shafts in her hands and stroked.

The men moaned in unison.

She leaned forward and kissed the tip of Greg's cock. She sucked him into her mouth, tickling the sensitive underside of his ridge.

After teasing him to full hardness, she bent and received Marc's large, thick cock into her mouth. He tasted different from Greg, more musky, but just as good. She took him to the base of his impressive cock, relaxing her throat to take him all.

She suckled the tip, dipping into the tiny hole, and was

rewarded by a taste of precome. Quivering with lust, she released Marc and returned to Greg.

She slid her tongue down his shaft, peppering it with tiny kisses and quick licks. She cupped his balls, playing with them before lowering her mouth to each one, suckling and laving.

Then she returned to Marc's cock. She sucked it into her mouth, slowly, inch by inch, until she'd taken it all again.

"Carrie," Marc said in a breathless voice, "that feels so good."

Desire pounded through her. She could barely catch her breath as she released Marc and took Greg's cock into her mouth again, all the way to the base. Her tongue ravaged the hard length, licking, stroking. She took all of him as she went down again and again.

God, she was turned on. Her pussy was wet and tight with need.

"Honey," warned Greg, "that feels too good."

Carrie rose to her knees and looked at the men. Her heart pounded unevenly. God, she couldn't believe she was going to experience her fantasy.

Five
. . . .

M arc patted the space between him and Greg. "It's your turn, Carrie."

Would Greg enjoy this? Would it change their relationship for the better . . . or for the worse? He nodded as if to reassure her that yes, he would share her—all the way—with Marc. Lust rippled through her. *Two men . . . oh yum!*

Carrie lay between the two men, trembling in fearful anticipation. Would this experience truly be what she wanted?

Marc and Greg stretched out on either side of her.

Marc leaned forward and cupped her breast, suckling the soft peak and laving it to hardness with his tongue. Then Greg cupped her other breast, kneading it gently. Then his mouth encircled her nipple.

Heat flooded her as Marc and Greg played with her breasts, their hands drifting down her rib cage, over her hips, down the insides of her thighs, then up again.

She squirmed and moaned, loving the feel of their lips, their hands and soon . . . their cocks.

Carrie's eyes drifted closed and she just enjoyed all the sensations. Two hands were good, but day-amn, four were better. A finger diddled her clit, then parted the folds of her pussy and dipped inside.

"Oh, God. Oh, yes!" she moaned.

Both men pressed against her, and she felt the thick lengths of their penises press into her thighs.

Now *two* fingers teased her pussy as both lovers suckled her nipples. The embers of her lust burst into ravaging flames that burned through her, heating to combustible levels.

"Take me," she whispered. "Both of you."

"Have you ever had anal sex, Carrie?" asked Marc.

"No," she admitted. "But I want you both inside me." She quivered at the very *idea* of two lovers penetrating her. What would it be like for real?

"We need to get you ready," said Marc. "I want you to get on top of Greg and lift your beautiful ass up for me."

She did as he directed. Her nipples scraped her husband's chest as her rear end hovered in the air, waiting for Marc's preparation.

From the corner of her eye, she saw him leave the bed and open the nightstand drawer. He put on a condom, tossing the foil packet back into the drawer. Then he removed a huge tube of lube.

She looked at Greg. Fear and excitement wound through her as she leaned down and kissed him. His tongue played with hers, and she let herself return to the game, to the fantasy.

The plastic tip of lubricant was inserted into her anus. She tensed as she felt the cold gel fill her. The reality of her sexual adventure walloped her. Was she really going to allow Marc to fuck her anally while Greg fucked her pussy?

She looked at Marc over her shoulder. "I'm not sure I can do this."

"Yes, you can." He tossed the tube onto the night stand. He smiled and then he *stuck his finger into her ass!* She yelped.

Marc chuckled. "This is for you, Carrie. All for you."

Greg was ready for her, his hard cock pressed against her stomach. His eyes were glazed with passion. The whole experience had turned him on, not off, as she had feared.

As Marc stretched her anal opening, Greg rolled her nipples between his fingers. Pleasure sparked through her.

"Take his cock," ordered Marc.

She lowered her pussy onto Greg's cock and used her inner muscles to stroke him.

He groaned.

Greg held on to her hips and executed smooth, long strokes while Marc played with her ass. She gave herself over to the sensations.

Then she felt Marc fit the head of his cock against her

ass. She sucked in a breath, her gaze flying to Greg's. He was in full-blown lust. He kept fucking her, and every time he bumped her clit, she felt her bliss peak higher and higher.

Marc leaned forward, working his big cock into her ass.

"It burns," said Carrie.

"Push back as I push in."

Greg stopped moving, and Carrie wiggled her ass back as much as she could. Marc slowly seated himself in her canal. Her ass tissues quivered and burned. The pressure was intense. Two cocks filled her and she wouldn't be surprised if the men could feel each other's members rubbing together.

She sucked in a few deep breaths. Her body trembled. Sensations rioted through her. God. Oh, God.

Greg thrust into her pussy. His hands moved to her shoulders; Marc's hands clamped on her hips. She kissed Greg, her tongue matching the slow rhythm of his cock.

Marc caught their rhythm, and soon, his cock was working in and out of her ass with same urgent cadence.

Greg bucked under her, his cock pumping faster. He was panting and straining, his face tight as he hurtled toward release.

They all fucked one another, sweating and groaning. Her breasts scraped Greg's chest and her buttocks slapped against Marc's hips.

"More!" cried Carrie. "Fuck me harder! Make me come!"

Their movements were frantic now, and the feel of Marc

plowing her ass and Greg fucking her pussy sent Carrie into a mind-blowing orgasm.

The pleasure ignited, burned, and took her to the stars. She floated in the waves of heat, trying to catch her breath.

Still, the men fucked her.

She had barely caught her breath when she felt Greg tense. He thrust deeply inside her, groaning as he came. His cock pulsed inside her.

Then Greg's cock slipped out of her. Marc's movements forced her clit to slide along the ridge of Greg's half-hard penis.

Carrie captured Greg's lips, warring with his tongue, feeling the rise of another orgasm. Oh, God.

Her clit throbbed, her second orgasm a few strokes away. "I'm coming!" cried Marc.

His cock throbbed against her sensitive ass tissues and she flew over the edge again, shuddering and breathless, collapsing onto Greg's chest.

Six

· · · · · · · ·

The next evening

Carrie held Greg's hand as they walked along the beach. Just minutes ago, they had indulged in a midnight swim, splashing and teasing each other.

Their bathing suits were still wet, but they didn't care.

"Would you ever want to do it again?" asked Greg.

Carrie stopped walking and looked at him. "Make love to two men?"

Greg nodded.

"I had the most wonderful fantasy, a fantasy that you made come true. I don't need to experience it again, honey. I have you. You're all I want." She cupped his face and kissed him. "Happy anniversary."

I Only Have
Eyes for You

· ·

Voyeur Village

One hundred lush acres on our Isle of Fetishes is devoted to our Voyeur Village.

If you relish watching others take pleasure—or you like others watching you get pleasure—then the village is the perfect place for you.

We have two designated beaches for nude sunbathing and skinny-dipping. All of our pools are clothing optional.

We highly recommend you make reservations for Gaze, our intimate supper club, which offers you sensual delights not only for your palate, but for your eyes.

And remember, at Voyeur Village, what you see . . . is what you get.

One
·······

Jake Malone inhaled the salty scent of ocean air as he re-
adjusted his position under the palm tree. His rear end
throbbed from sitting too long on the sand. Grit had crept
inside his wet swim trunks and abraded his skin.

The sun had risen in its usual glory, spreading orange
and yellow filaments across the tapestry of the topaz water.
It was too early in the morning for most guests staying at the
exclusive Voyeur Village, so the beach was deserted.

He loved being outdoors just before the day started. Usually, he was slinging a canvas bag onto his Harley and jump-
ing on the well-worn seat, riding to the next town. He never
stayed anywhere for long. The road was his mistress, seductively beckoning.

And he always answered that bitch's call.

But on this island, he didn't have his bike or a road or even a town. Last month, his brother had called him and given him the vacation. Maybe *foisted* was a better description.

"I was supposed to go with Tabitha, but we're over, man, and I don't feel like hanging around a meat market."

"Since when?"

"Hey, I have a broken heart. What's your excuse?"

"I go only where my muse takes me."

"Aw, shit. Don't give me that soulful crap, Jake. You like getting laid as much as the next guy, and this place is all about sexual conquests."

"Fine," said Jake, relenting.

Jake's whole life was a vacation. He was a photographer who traveled the world. He was beholden to no one, and he liked it that way. But who could resist a paid vacation to a tropical island where women were plentiful and willing?

A tropical breeze ruffled the edges of his much-read copy of Jack Kerouac's *On the Road.* It had been his companion longer than anything, than anyone, in his life. Except Mike. But other than his only sibling, all he'd ever had was his motorcycle and his need to keep moving.

Jake closed the book he hadn't really been reading, anyway. Suddenly restless, he rose and dusted sand off his legs. The swim he'd taken earlier had stretched his muscles and burned off the beer calories he'd consumed the night before. Man, he was starving. He started down the beach and headed toward the hotel. Maybe he'd get some breakfast and take in some of the sights. He'd heard about a clothing-optional cruise that took guests to a private cove for snorkeling and other, less tame activities. Or he could—

"Excuse me!" cried a female voice. "Sir? Hello!"

Jake looked around, trying to determine where the voice was coming from and if it was targeted at him.

He spotted the woman in a small grove of palms and bushes. She was backed against a tall palm, somehow snagged on it. When he got closer he realized two things:

She wore only a black lace bra and matching thong.

She was tied to the tree.

His cock perked up instantly. Her breasts were spilling out of the bra, and the panties had shifted so that he could see the smooth line of her pussy.

Whoa.

There wasn't a breakfast anywhere on this island that could compete with the buffet this woman offered. She had the reddest hair he'd ever seen and there was lots of it, wavy and long. She was all lush curves, and she radiated pure sex. He wanted to fill his hands with her, take her into his mouth, part her thighs and slide into her luscious cunt.

He wanted to feast on her.

Defiant green eyes stared him down, but he saw the tear tracks on her cheeks.

"Who did this?" he asked softly. "Are you hurt? Did they . . . do anything to you?"

"I wish! I am tied to a tree because I'm an idiot. Nobody

hurt me. My pride is used to the battering, believe me. But I just thought that if you come to an island that's all about sex, then it would be possible to get sex. I was wrong."

"How could you be wrong?" *I will give you sex. As much as you want.*

"Could you untie my hands? I've been here a while, evaluating my pathetic life while my hands went numb."

Jake worked out the knots and the rope fell away. The woman rubbed her hands together. She flashed him a smile that revealed dimples.

He felt as though he'd been knocked on his ass. His pulse stuttered and his libido revved into high gear.

"Thanks," she said. "I appreciate the rescue."

"Believe me, it was my pleasure. I'm Jake."

"Rhiannon."

Even her name was beautiful. He wanted to . . . to . . . to lick her.

"Well, I have to go. I've had enough of *paradise.*"

"You're leaving?"

One red brow quirked. "Yeah."

"You're the first interesting person I've met since I got here," protested Jake.

"You're such a cute liar. I've met a lot of those recently." She put her hands on her hips—her lovely, lovely hips—and stared at him. Her breasts jiggled enticingly, giving the impression they might fall out of their lacy restraints. "I saved up for a whole year to afford three days here. On a waitress salary, that's difficult to do. I leave tomorrow morning, and let me tell you, this place has been nothing but disappointment."

"You want to tell me what happened?"

"Yeah, sure. Why not? I mean, who are you, but a complete stranger?"

She sighed deeply, which caused more breast jiggling. He pried his eyes away from her chest. Luckily, she wasn't looking at him, but staring at the ground.

"Well, you untied me, so I guess I owe you some kind of explanation. Last night, I went to Watchers—it's this dance club. I cage danced and loved it. Felt sexy as hell. This guy introduces himself, gets all cozy with me, and arranges a little rendezvous. I show up, and he gets my clothes off, ties me to the palm tree, then takes a picture with his cell phone.

"Him and his pals have this little game they play. I got him fifty points and a round of beers because I fall into the fat-chick category." Fury vibrated in every word. Her finger speared the air. "He left me tied to the tree because I threatened to rip off his balls. Chickenhearted bastard."

"You're not fat," Jake pointed out. "You should report that asshole to a Safety Agent."

She rolled her eyes. "Do you know how many people are on this island? You know damned well he didn't tell me his real name. Oh, screw him. And thanks for saying I'm not fat. You have a kind heart or bad eyes."

Rhiannon bent over and Jake nearly lost his ability to

breathe. Her ass was perfect. He fisted his hands so that he wouldn't reach out and caress its delectable roundness.

When she stood up and turned around, she had her clothes, purse, and high heels bundled in her arms.

"Let me take you to breakfast, Rhiannon."

The idea did not thrill her if the expression on her face was any indication.

"Consider it an apology on behalf of moronic males everywhere."

She chuckled, but shook her head. "I've had all the fun I can stand. But thanks."

Jake opened his arms in a beseeching gesture, giving her his most soulful look.

"Oh, you're good." She stepped forward and her eyes went wide. Everything she'd just gathered went flying into the air as she tripped. She fell forward into Jake's outstretched arms.

His hand slid up her thigh as she knocked him down. Jake wrapped his other arm around her waist and felt her hands clutch his shoulders. He fell backward, smacking into the gritty beach so hard his lungs nearly collapsed.

Rhiannon lifted her head and glared at him. "Would you be so kind as to remove your hand from my buttock?"

He flexed automatically on the nicely rounded flesh. "Do I have to?"

Her green eyes were flecked with gold. She had ivory skin and a full mouth, the kind that begged to be kissed. "You're incorrigible."

"Yeah. I'm lots of other things, too."

"Horny must be one of them."

Her amused words infiltrated his lust-fogged thoughts. She was referring to the hard-on that pressed against her stomach.

"I'm very, very, *very* attracted to you."

"Wow." She rolled off, stumbling to her feet. "Was the breakfast going to be in bed?"

"Only if you want it to be." He stood up and touched her elbow. It was time for bold action. If he let her out of his sight, she'd be off the island before he could track her down again.

"Maybe you just need convincing." The rich timbre of Jake's voice had a sensual quality that made Rhiannon's nerves prickle. The lazy, intent glittering in his hazel eyes warned her, but before she could protest, he lowered his head and pressed warm, soft lips against her mouth.

Shocked into stillness, Rhiannon didn't move—not even when Jake pulled her closer and deepened the kiss. He tasted of coffee and mint, and his lips did not demand, but coaxed. Her breasts pressed against the hard planes of his chest and her nipples hardened.

Damn, it had been a long time since she'd been kissed. And she couldn't remember the experience ever being like *this*. His tongue flicked the corner of her mouth and a jolt of electricity zapped the pit of her stomach. With that opening salvo, he invaded, his tongue tangling with hers.

Heat coiled in her belly and sparked every nerve ending. Arousal liquefied her body, clouded her mind, and dissolved her doubts.

This was what she'd been looking for at Fantasyland. This experience, this feeling, this need to be fulfilled.

He stopped kissing her, his breathing erratic as he looked at her and grinned. She hung on to Jake's shoulders, trying to calm her galloping heart rate. Feeling shaky, Rhiannon let go of him and touched her mouth, feeling the swelling of lips that still throbbed.

God, he was so cute. No, "cute" wasn't the right word. He was freaking gorgeous.

Jake's face was all sharp angles, softened only by the fullness of his mouth and the warmth sparkling in his hazel eyes. His longish blond hair was pulled into a ponytail. She wondered what it looked like down . . . what it might feel like in her hands. Muscled. God, he was muscled. The fit of his swim trunks would be declared illegal in some states.

"Thanks for saving me," she finally managed to say. "Twice."

He clasped her wrists and tugged her forward. "The first rescue was free, Rhiannon. But the second one . . . well, you'll have to pay for it."

"Pay for it?"

"Yep."

Her heart trilled. Was that the beat of fear? Or of longing? For a moment, she entertained the idea of repaying him in a way that would rock both their worlds. She hadn't been with anyone since Chad dumped her. Twenty-six months was a long time to go without a real penis. But hell, that was why she had booked a vacation at Fantasyland. So far, her daydreams of amazing sex with a dishy guy had turned into nightmares.

Did she have the courage to just . . . well, to just fuck Jake? Her pussy clenched—the wetness in her panties a testament to her body's vote on the subject. Instead, she broke his finger lock on her wrists and stepped back. "I don't owe you anything."

"*Rhiannon.*" Desire flared in his eyes. He held up his hands in supplication. "All I wanted was another kiss."

Well, what could one more kiss hurt? She nodded, anticipation thrumming through her.

To her shock, the crazy man dropped to his knees and grasped her hips.

"What are you doing, Jake?"

"I said I wanted a kiss. But I didn't say where."

Two

· · · · · · ·

"Y ou're not seri—"

Jake pressed his mouth to the vee of her thighs. Rhiannon almost fell over. *Oh. My. God.* His accuracy was uncanny. Shock and pleasure reverberated in her core as she tried to form an objection.

The wet warmth of his lips penetrated the lace of her thong. His breath fluttered through the barriers and ghosted down her pussy. She grabbed his shoulders—to push him away, of course. Instead, she held on to steady herself, to readjust a little to the left.

As promised, he kissed her—a firm push of his lips against her clit. Then he pulled away and looked up at her.

"I want to taste you, Rhiannon. Let me pleasure you."

"Here? *Now?*" she squeaked.

"Why not?" Jake eased her panties down her thighs, exposing her smooth, hairless pussy. "That's a beautiful sight."

He wiggled his tongue across her slit.

The feminine spice of her sex was ambrosia. Jake loved the taste and smell of a woman's pussy. He couldn't wait to lick and nibble her tender flesh; he couldn't wait to plunge his tongue into her delicious cunt. Just thinking about Rhiannon's come filling his mouth made his already-hard cock quake.

He leaned forward and kissed the spot just above her crease. The mere pressing of his lips against her smooth, warm skin sent sparks of lust shooting through him. Dragging his tongue down the slender line, he feasted on her plump, slick flesh.

He dipped inside, tasting her feminine essence. Then he skimmed his tongue along her slick folds until he reached her clitoris. He flicked the swollen nub.

She moaned.

He slid two fingers inside her wet heat and curled them upward.

"Oh, God," she cried. "What . . . is . . . that?"

Bingo. *Houston, I've found the G-spot.* He stroked that bump eagerly. He looked up and noted with satisfaction that her eyes were closed and her face was flushed.

Then he captured her clit and sucked on it.

Rhiannon came.

He gladly accepted the assault of her fingers digging into his skull and the pumping of her hips as her pussy sucked at his fingers.

He resettled his hands onto her ass and gorged on the nirvana creaming her hot pussy. He could've stayed there forever, licking her and tasting her, but she broke free and stumbled backward.

She stared at him, her eyes still glazed with lust, her body glistening in the sunlight. She tugged up her thong as she watched him struggle to his feet. Jake's entire body was quivering with lust. His cock pressed painfully against the netting in his swim trunks.

Jake didn't want their liaison to be over. He wanted to worship Rhiannon like the goddess she was. He wanted to kiss every inch of flesh, memorize every curve, and if she granted him the right, plunge his aching cock into her tight little pussy.

"Are you okay?" he asked.

"That was . . . phenomenal."

"It doesn't have to be over." He wanted to draw her into his embrace, but she looked skittish. He opted for smoothing a loose curl away from her cheek. "Please stay, Rhiannon. How about dinner tonight? Give me a chance to be your fantasy. You're already mine."

"You're so full of shit." She looked away, nibbling her lower lip. Then she met his gaze. "Okay. Dinner."

"Eight o'clock. I'll meet you in the hotel lobby." He picked up the book he'd dropped into the sand. "I'm in room five-oh-eight if you want *anything* before then."

Her lips hitched into a grin. "Anything?"

"I'm your willing slave," he said. He took her hand and kissed her knuckles. "Until tonight."

61

* * *

Jake woke from his nap. He looked at the digital alarm clock on the nightstand. Hell, it was barely four. He'd kept himself busy most of the day, taking photos, eating at the buffet, swimming at the pool, but every activity was filled with thoughts of Rhiannon.

As his hard-on attested, he'd been dreaming of lips and sighs and beautiful green eyes. Rhiannon. Would she show up for their date? Or had she packed her bags and left?

God, she was just so luscious.

Jake threw off the covers. He might as well raid the suite's refrigerator and catch some television. Four more hours seemed like an eternity. Ignoring the robe draped over the dresser, he left the bedroom and went into the kitchenette. Goose pimples rose on his flesh, but he liked the cool air.

Opening the fridge, he peered at the sparse offerings. Hmm. Maybe he should order room service instead.

Someone knocked on the door.

His heart turned over in his chest. Rhiannon? Please, God! He ducked into the bedroom to grab the robe, which he tugged on hurriedly. He rubbed a hand through his hair. Damn it. He probably had a terrible case of bed head. He'd taken a shower before his nap and hadn't bothered to blow it dry.

Another knock, this one more tentative. Without bothering to look through the peephole, he flung open the door.

Rhiannon wore a pair of tight jeans and a glitzy halter top. Her feet were clasped in zebra-print high heels. Big gold hoops dangled from her lobes.

"I decided I wanted anything."

"Thank God!" He moved out of the way and she sashayed inside. He put the DO NOT DISTURB card on the door before shutting it.

"Nice place." She dropped her purse onto the couch and wandered around the room.

Decorated in dark blue and silver, from the navy carpet to the striped couch, the living room looked both luxurious and comfortable. While cherrywood end tables, each with a thin silver lamp, graced either end of the couch, there wasn't a coffee table or an entertainment center housing a TV and stereo.

Floor-to-ceiling glass made up the wall separating the bedroom from the living room. On the far left was the narrow doorless entry into the bedroom. The couch was in direct view of the huge circular bed. Someone sitting on it could easily watch whoever might be lolling around the mattress.

"That's an interesting feature." She looked at him as she moistened her lips. Her little pink tongue roved over her bottom lip. God, that mouth was sexy.

"I'm sorry I woke you up," she said, not sounding sorry at all. "Hell, I wasn't sure I could work up the nerve."

She went to the sliding-glass doors that led to the balcony with its ocean view. He followed her onto the small terrace. They stood side by side and stared at the undulating water. The air felt damp and smelled salty. The waves slapped at the shore in a slow rhythm.

Jake turned to her.

Her eyes flared with desire and his blood stirred. Jake

grasped her arms and pulled her into his embrace. She looked at him, wide-eyed, anticipation and lust colliding in the depths of her gaze. He wanted her. She wanted him. It could be just that simple, if they let it.

He kissed her.

She responded passionately, her lips melting against his as her tongue dipped into his mouth.

He quivered. God, she made him hot. She made him want. He suspected one taste of Rhiannon would never be enough.

Her hands dove into the robe. Her palms coasted down his stomach, seeking the evidence of his desire. She gripped his cock and stroked.

"Oh, hell." He pulled away, panting. "Don't do that, baby, or I'll come. I've been thinking about you all day."

"I want you," she said in a husky voice. "Desperately."

"Then you better get out of those clothes."

She smiled, her eyes glittering with excitement. "That's exactly what I plan to do."

In the living room, Rhiannon settled Jake on the couch. She pushed the coffee table to the side so that she would have room for her performance.

She toed off her shoes, then wiggled out of her jeans. She heard his sharp intake of breath when he caught a glimpse of her red lace thong. She stuck her feet back into the heels, then looked around.

On the left end table was a CD player. Rhiannon dug

into her purse and pulled out a case. Popping the CD into the slot, she picked out the song she wanted.

As the opening to Avril Lavigne's "Keep Holding On" soared through the speakers, Rhiannon took her position, arms up and gaze on Jake. She spun around, sliding her hands down her sides, then over her ass.

She bent over.

"God in heaven."

Jake's strained voice filtered through Avril's insistence to keep holding on. Rhiannon grinned. God, she loved to dance. To show off. She did yoga every day and had even taken a few "stripper aerobics" classes. Of course, being a healthy "big" girl didn't mean much in a world filled with skinny people. But Jake didn't seem to notice or, for that matter, care that she was a size fourteen.

She was holding his attention, making him look, but not touch. Yeah, she was making him want her badly while keeping herself just out of reach.

Jake now had a prime view of her buttocks. The thong denied him a view of her pussy, but the temptation was there, covered by thin red lace.

Rolling back up, she wiggled around in a tight circle once, twice, and then stopped, giving him a side view. She drew the halter over her head, rubbing the material on her breasts—clad in a matching red lace bra—and stomach before dropping it.

Once again, she bent over.

Placing her palms flat on the floor, she braced her arms, then brought up her legs. She drifted into a backbend, then collapsed to the floor and rolled to her side.

Now on her stomach, she brought her head and feet up until they nearly met. Then she pressed down again, and pushed up so that her body formed a triangle.

She popped up to her feet and undulated toward him. His eyes were dazed, his hands clenching the couch cushions. Oh, yeah. His hard-on tented the robe.

The song was nearing its end, so she let her fingers drift down between her breasts. She unsnapped the bra's front clip and cupped her tits, denying him the pleasure of seeing the material fall away.

She turned her back to him, dancing, and took off the bra, slinging it to the floor. As Avril promised one last time that "we'll make it through," Rhiannon faced Jake. Her hands glided from her breasts, down her stomach, and over her hips. She hooked her thumbs in the red panties as the last note faded away.

For a long moment, Jake just stared at her. Her heart pounded and her pussy was already wet. She loved how he looked at her, as if she were the last chocolate bar in the candy store.

"Well," she prompted, "what do you think?"

"Take off those panties and I'll show you."

Three

G rinning, Rhiannon wiggled out of the thong. Her heart thudded from both exertion and sexual need.

Jake took her hand and pulled her onto the couch. His lips captured hers, his tongue slipping inside to ratchet up the heat. She melted into his arms and deepened their contact. He tasted like peppermint. She could smell the light scent of soap and the musky scent of sex.

Desire and need streaked through her, pooling wet and hot between her thighs. Reaching between them, she stroked his cock through the robe.

Rhiannon kissed his jaw, dragging her lips down his neck, then back up again. Her fingers curled under the edges of the robe, which she opened to reveal his delicious body.

He sure was built. The man had nice abs. Brown hair

lightly furred his pectorals and stomach. With lips and tongue, Rhiannon worked her way to his pectorals, taking a detour to one coin-sized areola and its tiny, hard peak. She tugged it between her teeth, flicking the tip rapidly. He groaned, his hands wrapping in her hair as she attacked his other nipple and gave it the same treatment.

"Oh, Rhiannon," he murmured, "you feel so good."

She moved farther down his chest, exploring the muscled ridges of his stomach with hands and mouth.

Slipping to the floor, she knelt between his legs. She grasped his thick, hard shaft, loving the feel of it against her palm.

Cupping his balls, she squeezed lightly as she licked his mushroom head, sucking it into her mouth. She swirled her tongue around the rim, flicking the tiny bumps on the underside.

His breathing went ragged and his thighs tensed.

Rhiannon's heart pounded frantically as lust thickened in her belly. She wanted Jake desperately. Her body hummed with need, with heat.

The musky scent of his sex excited her. She went down on him all the way, sucking his manhood to the base as she fondled his sac.

He nearly launched off the couch, but managed to reseat himself. One of his hands clutched at the couch arm, while the other pressed against her skull.

Rhiannon was too impatient to mess around with

pretty seduction. She gave him a down-and-dirty blow job, lubing his cock with her tongue as she went down on him again and again. He pumped into her mouth, his cock banging against the back of her throat, but she took him, took him all.

"Baby, I'm going to come."

Oh, no, he wasn't. Not without her.

She dug into her purse and took out a condom. He sucked air through clenched teeth as she rolled it on.

Then she crawled onto his lap and he helped her guide his swollen member into her pussy. For a moment, she simply sat there and enjoyed the feel of his penetration as he stretched her, as he filled her.

Jake cupped her breasts, brushing the hard peaks with his thumbs. He sucked one into his mouth, licking it rapidly with his tongue.

Pleasure sparked through her.

"Oh, yeah," she moaned. "I like that. Mmm."

He switched nipples, sucking one and twisting the other. Fire raced from her breasts to her pussy. Awash in sensations, she seemed to lose the ability to breathe, to think.

"Fuck me," she whispered.

Jake didn't need a second invitation. He gripped her hips, his gaze on hers as he thrust upward. Her knees dug into the couch cushions as she rode him.

"I can't last," he said. "You feel too good."

As Jake pounded into her, Rhiannon cupped her own

tits and pulled on her nipples. She twisted her peaks until the pleasure-pain started a rumbling avalanche.

"Harder," she begged. "Please. Fuck me hard. Yes, oh yes . . . Jake!"

Her bliss erupted and shot her into the stars. Vaguely, she felt Jake's deep thrust, his groan intertwining with her low cries, and then he came, too.

She floated back to earth.

"You're amazing," murmured Jake as he wrapped his arms around her.

Rhiannon stood in the bedroom, looking at the rumpled sheets. The walls were painted a pale shade of blue and all the furniture was big, chunky, and dark.

Jake entered the room, crossing to her. He studied her until she squirmed under his perusal. "You're safe with me." He brushed his knuckles across her cheek. "You can trust me."

"Can I? I don't know." She pressed a trembling hand against her belly. "I don't understand why I feel this way, why I came here."

"Yes, you do."

Before she could try to deny his words, Jake put a finger to her lips. His gaze was all heat, all possession. What had she gotten herself into? He was too much for her.

"Rhiannon." He tapped her lips. "Stay with me. You don't need to think about anything except what's happening right now."

He stepped behind her and placed his hands on her shoulders. He kneaded out the kinks, smoothed away tightness, helped her relax. She sighed deeply and leaned into the massage. Slowly, Rhiannon became aware of the change in Jake's touches, how his fingers stroked long lines down her back and up her arms. His warm breath stirred the hair at the nape of her neck.

She stilled, afraid he wouldn't move—afraid he would. An aeon passed. Then Jake's hands trailed up her rib cage, stopping under her breasts. She felt the barest touch of his fingers. She moaned softly.

"You are so sexy," Jake whispered. His lips found the curve of her neck, and his tongue traced a path to her ear. "Everything about you turns me on."

Wow. Oh *wow*. Rhiannon wanted his mouth, his hands. She tried to turn into his embrace, but he stalled her. "Don't move."

"Jake. Please . . ."

"What do you want, Rhiannon?"

"You."

He chuckled. "Be more specific."

How simple to ask for what she wanted. Yet she couldn't get her lips to form the request. It wasn't like she wanted anything difficult or strange. A *kiss*. How hard was it to ask to be kissed?

Really damn hard. A kiss was a promise—an offer of affection or a tortured begging. It could be so lovely or so disappointing. And Jake knew how to kiss. God, did he ever.

Jake turned her to face him and her eyes flew open. After

a moment, she managed to stop acting like a twit. She squared her shoulders and met his gaze.

"What do you want?" he asked again.

"Kiss me," she whispered.

Her heart doubled its already-frantic beat as he lowered his mouth to hers. He stopped a breath away—his tongue flicked out. Tendrils of longing wound through her as he traced the inner curve of her lower lip. Oh how she wanted him to plunder, to take. But he was gentle, coaxing . . . tormenting her with mere flashes of sensation.

Finally, he claimed her lips fully. His mouth was warm and tasted faintly of toothpaste. He deepened the kiss, pulling her closer, stoking her desire.

She felt shattered and whole at the same time.

Jake pulled away, his heated gaze filled with a hunger that weakened her knees. He pressed his mouth at the hollow of her throat. She inhaled sharply and clenched his shoulders. Jake nipped kisses up her neck, flicking his tongue on her warm skin. Desire twisted inside her, a spiraling need that claimed her until all she could feel, all she could *breathe*, was Jake.

"I want you, Rhiannon," he said in a jagged voice. He cupped her face and feathered kisses along her jaw. Relentless, he again took her lips in a fierce possession, showing her with his mouth what he wanted to do with her body.

Jake groaned when he felt Rhiannon's fingertips lightly brush his cock. He gathered her close, kissing her, touching her, stroking her. He looked at her breasts. Firm and beautiful, the coral tips puckered, so Jake bent and took a nipple in his mouth, teasing it, pulling and sucking. Rhiannon's moan nearly broke him.

Her hands were everywhere, on his chest, in his hair, on his arms and shoulders . . . on his painful arousal. She drove him wild, distracted him from the gentle seduction he wanted to give her.

He took her to the bed, laid her down, and covered her, nuzzling her neck as his hands roved her curves.

It was time to claim her.

He spread apart her cunt and licked the glistening flesh. He couldn't resist teasing her clit. She sucked in a startled breath, clutching at his hair. Grasping her ass, he pulled her to his mouth . . . sucking . . . licking . . . kissing. Then he shoved his tongue into her pussy, tasting her sweet musk, drinking the evidence of her desire. He thrust over and over, until her cunt was soaked with her juices and she was panting and squirming.

He savored her spice, bringing her closer and closer to a peak.

Then he withdrew, dragging his lips over her stomach, between the valley of her breasts, to her throat.

"Hurry," she begged hoarsely. "Fuck me. I want your cock inside me."

Her hands curled around his buttocks and she rubbed her slick cunt along his cock. His balls tightened. His cock was so sensitive to her movements, he could come any second. He sucked in a steadying breath.

"Wait." He reached into the drawer of the nightstand and pulled out an unopened box of condoms. It took precious seconds to rip open the container, get a condom out of its package, and roll the rubber onto his throbbing shaft.

He entered her slowly, groaning at the tight, wonderful feel of her pussy. She sighed in satisfaction, her fingers trailing across his back.

His heart pounded fiercely as he looked at her. Her gorgeous red hair spilled over her creamy shoulders. Her breasts gleamed with sweat; the coral nipples beckoned his mouth once again.

"I can't get enough of you."

She moaned and arched against him, offering her breasts to his eager mouth. As he teased her sensitive nipples, he increased his strokes.

Her fingernails dug into his shoulders.

"That's it, sweetheart," he said softly. "Oh, God, I can't hold it. You feel too good, Rhiannon!"

She shattered around him, milking his cock into explosive pleasure. For a long moment, he rode the wave, losing his breath and his sight.

Then he managed to reengage his lungs and opened his eyes. Her wide smile revealed those heavenly dimples. He swallowed the knot suddenly clogging his throat. He wasn't sure that a mere night with her would be enough. Even now, with his balls emptied and his body limp, he didn't want to let her go.

"Breathing room," she said, laughing.

He slid to her side and drew her into his arms.

"Still two hours until our dinner date," she said. Her eyes went coy. "Whatever shall we do?"

"Hmm." He wiped beads of sweat off her temples. "How do you feel about water, soap . . . and me?"

Four
· · · · · · · ·

Jake joined Rhiannon under the hot spray. She took the small bar of soap and washed him slowly, thoroughly from head to toe.

As she washed his penis, she cupped his balls, squeezing them lightly with her sudsy hands.

Jake watched her, his gaze already lustful. His cock hardened under her cleansing technique.

"Time to rinse." He turned toward the pulsating water and scrubbed off the soap. Then he backed her against the wall and pushed his cock into the wet vee of her thighs. She held his face in her palms and kissed him. He accepted the tenderness of her gesture, his hands cupping her breasts. Rhiannon moaned.

He leaned down and suckled her nipples. The water beat

down on them, but she didn't care about washing up anymore. Jake lifted one of her legs, then guided his cock into her pussy. She shuddered at the sensual contact.

Rhiannon clutched his shoulders, her gaze held hostage by his. He thrust hard and deep, grunting and groaning, his teeth clenched as he took his pleasure, as he gave *her* pleasure. Her nails dug into Jake's shoulders as he fucked her. This mating wasn't gentle at all. It was pure carnality, lovemaking without words, without limits.

Again and again, Jake slammed into her. Her ass slapped against the tile and her moans mingled with his. He plunged deeply, his fingers jabbing into her thighs, his eyes on hers as he brought her to a shattering orgasm.

"Rhiannon!"

He pulled out, grabbing his cock and stroking it to final orgasm. Even as she recovered from her own pleasure, she watched him come. He squeezed his shaft, jerking it hard. Semen shot in white arcs, landing on her stomach, thighs, and the shower stall.

"Jesus." Jake gathered her into his arms, kissing her. "You make me so hot. I've never wanted anyone like you."

She didn't believe him, but she thought he was nice for telling such wonderful lies.

They held each other, breathing hard, shuddering under the tepid water. Then Jake cleaned her, even washing her hair.

If she wasn't careful, if she didn't remember that this was

Fantasyland and not reality, she just might start falling for Jake.

When they arrived at the supper club called Gaze, Jake studied the nondescript building. It was square, white, and windowless. The only indication that they were at the right place was the blue neon sign above the double doors.

A blond hostess led them into a foyer with teak walls, a marble floor, and low lighting. Several other couples waited there, as well. After a few more people arrived, the hostess opened another set of double doors and they all filed inside.

The room was square and plain. Its only decoration was the soft glow of blue lighting. Long, cushioned benches lined the left and right walls. Every five feet was a large, square table.

The guests were escorted to their designated table and sat hip to hip on the bench. Inset in the middle of the table was a bucket filled with ice and a bottle of champagne. There were fluted glasses for the champagne and two folded cloth napkins, but no silverware or plates.

"No menus?" asked Rhiannon.

"The chef chooses everything—from the appetizer to the dessert. It's always different," the hostess said.

At least forty feet yawned between the guests and the other side of the room. In the center of the bare floor was a long, low stage, where Jake assumed the show would be performed.

He tugged the champagne out of its bucket, noting that its cork was already gone. The staff probably opened all the champagne bottles right before seating everyone.

He poured the golden liquid into the glasses, then returned the bottle and picked up his glass. "To new fantasies."

Rhiannon smiled and tapped his glass with hers; then they both sipped. The bubbles tickled his tongue and the dry taste had a hint of sweetness.

Doors opened on the far right side of the room. Women scantily clad in lingerie entered. They carried two plates each.

Jake only knew about Gaze from the brochure in his hotel room. He refused to give in to the temptation to stare. Instead he kept his eyes on the table and refused to look at the beautiful woman as she leaned over the table and deposited the two plates.

"My name is Monique," she said in a low voice dripping with a French accent. A small bowl of creamy dip was surrounded by baby carrots, slivers of zucchini, grape tomatoes, and crackers.

"For your pleasure, we have a creamy artichoke dip with organic vegetables and wheat crackers. Enjoy your appetizer, *mes amis.*"

Her beauty was facilitated by good bone structure and clever makeup. She appeared untouchable—the way a supermodel looked as she strutted on the catwalk. Dressed in a pink corset that was attached to black silk stockings, she wore a matching set of pink panties. Her stilettos were black and shiny. She smelled like jasmine and her smile appeared genuine, if a shade too perfect.

Rhiannon was so much more beautiful in comparison.

They made small talk as they ate their appetizers. Rhiannon was a waitress in Reno. She liked the work, liked Reno, and enjoyed studying the history of Nevada. "We're only twelve miles from Virginia City—that's where the Comstock Lode was found. Anyway, Reno is the real jewel. Have you ever been there?"

He shook his head.

"You've traveled all over the world, but you've never been to Reno? That's just wrong."

He smiled. "Consider it on my list of places to visit in the near future."

Monique returned to clear their plates and deliver their salads. She stacked their appetizer dishes and pushed them to the side. Then she placed two chilled bowls filled with crisp romaine lettuce and toppings and two silver forks in front of them.

"Tonight, we serve you Caesar salad with shaved Parmesan-Reggiano cheese, black olives, red onion slices, and quartered Romano tomatoes." Her baby blues gazed at him. "Do you find it to your liking, monsieur?"

"Uh, yeah. Thanks."

"And you, mademoiselle?"

"The salads look gorgeous," said Rhiannon. "And so do you."

The blonde's smile widened. "You are most kind." Then she whisked away the dishes.

"You really think she was pretty?" he asked. He let his gaze follow the blonde's twitching buttocks. She had a nice ass. Then he looked at his salad because he couldn't quite face Rhiannon.

"You may find this strange, Jake, but women do look at other women. Usually, we do it to figure out how we look in comparison. Is my ass smaller than hers? Do I have bigger boobs?" She pierced the salad with her fork and took a bite.

He glanced at her. "Is that why you looked at her?"

"I found her very attractive. She likes to be looked at—and so do I."

Jake nodded. "I'll look at you and anyone else until my eyes fall out if it'll make you happy."

"Good to know."

After they finished off their salads, he poured more champagne.

"Are you a voyeur?" she asked.

"Everyone's a voyeur to some extent."

She considered his words. "But not everyone is an exhibitionist."

"No. But you are."

"Yeah."

Monique returned to clear off their salad bowls and silverware. After she left, a waiter dressed in a tuxedo placed two steaming dishes of food before Rhiannon and Jake, along with steak knives and forks. "Tonight's feast is filet mignon and lobster tail served with steamed asparagus."

They enjoyed the food while Jake talked about his passion for photography and his trips to places like Brazil and Jamaica.

Minutes after they finished their meal, Monique reappeared. She once again removed their dishes, then set a plate between them filled with three types of cheese.

"We have Halloumi—which is folded cheese with mint; Stilton, which is handmade in Britain; and Tavor, an Israeli cheese that's a blend of sheep's and goat's milk."

"Looks wonderful," murmured Jake.

"How was your dinner?" Monique asked. Her gaze pingponged between him and Rhiannon.

"Fabulous," he said.

"Definitely," Rhiannon agreed.

The slow beat of drums filtered into the restaurant.

"Ah," said the waitress with a coy smile. "The show . . . it begins."

The blue lights went out, casting the entire place in darkness. The drumbeats increased as three people—painted in neon purple, pink, and green—emerged from the floor. Spotlights shone down on the dancers, highlighting the splashes of color on their bodies.

The two men spied the lone female and crept forward, as if intending to pounce on her. She twirled away. Every lithe movement and graceful leap was accentuated by the pounding music.

Rhiannon watched, riveted by the graceful moves of the lissome dancers.

Jake's hand crept into hers and held it tightly.

They watched the men chase the woman. They would almost catch her, but she would flit away, as illusive and beautiful as a butterfly. The music was frenetic and intense as the dancers ran and jumped, arms reaching, yet never quite touching.

Jake released her hand and trailed his fingers up her side. Her breath hitched as he dared to cup her breast. Her nipple hardened instantly. His hand dropped away, fingers stroking her rib cage to rest lightly on her hip.

The light touch of his fingers against her thigh was filled with erotic promise. Her heart skipped a beat and she waited, nearly breathless, to see where else he would touch her.

She watched the dancers, who increased her excitement. The woman had been caught. One man stood in front of her and the other behind her. Hands stroked neon-speckled flesh.

Jake's hand ventured under Rhiannon's dress. One finger dipped into her panties, stroking her clit. He leaned close and whispered, "Play with your breasts."

Was he seriously going to give her an orgasm in a restaurant full of people?

She cupped her breasts, rubbing her thumbs over her distended nipples. Desire skittered through her, arrowing straight to her pussy.

The drumbeat went crazy and the trio of dancers moved in a crazed rhythm. Back and forth, bodies surging and colliding as the music rose higher and higher.

Jake's whisper tickled Rhiannon's ear. "I love stroking your clit. I love making you come. Come for me, baby."

Rhiannon's lungs nearly collapsed. She twisted her nipples as his finger stroked her clit faster and faster.

The music hit a crescendo . . .

. . . and so did she. The orgasm burst, as sweet and hot as ripe berries picked on a summer day. She was panting heavily, unable to steady her own breathing. Jake removed his hand and her hands drifted away from her breasts.

The drumbeats faded away. The three people wrapped arms around one another, then sank slowly into the floor. The blue lights turned on, chasing away the darkness.

Jake looked at Rhiannon, smiling wickedly as he licked her essence off his finger. "You taste better than anything I've eaten tonight."

Oh, Lord, the man had a silver tongue. Rhiannon couldn't think of an appropriate response, so she said nothing.

Monique arrived with the same tuxedoed waiter. He cleared away the cheese plate. From a tray balanced on her hip, Monique placed two plates of tiramisu before them.

Then she set out two tiny cups of espresso. "Did you enjoy the show?"

"Yes," said Rhiannon. She wondered if she looked as orgasmic as she felt.

"And you, monsieur?"

"The best show ever."

Five
· · · · · · · ·

They walked along the deserted beach. The moon hung full and bright in the star-jeweled sky. The ocean gurgled contentedly as its foamy fingers tickled the shoreline.

Rhiannon held her handbag in one hand and her heels in the other.

"I'm still hard," complained Jake. He enchained her wrist. She dropped her heels as he brought her hand to the front of his pants. "That's what you do to me."

"Aw, poor baby."

She smiled, then looked around. "There's a palm tree. Why don't you fulfill a fantasy gone awry?"

"My pleasure." He scooped up her heels and hurried with her to the lone palm tree.

"Wrap your arms around it."

Rhiannon dropped her purse. He tossed her shoes next to it. Then she bent over and wrapped her arms around the scratchy bark of the tree.

She watched him take off his belt.

Jake pinned her wrists together and wrapped the belt around them, snaking the leather into a knot.

He took position behind her. He flipped up her dress and dragged her red thong down to her ankles.

"W-what are you doing?"

"What's wrong, baby? You afraid someone will see us?" His hands coasted up her thighs and over her buttocks. Excitement raced up her spine. Jake knew her hot buttons, all right.

She heard him unzip his pants; then she felt the ridge of his hard cock pressed against her ass. She bit her lower lip as he gripped her hips and slid his shaft between her thighs. He pierced her slick folds, nudging her entrance.

"You're so wet." He reached around and stroked her clit. "Do you want me to fuck you, baby?"

"Yes." She moaned as he fit the head of his cock inside her. But he didn't move. She wiggled back, but he clenched her hips to keep her in that teasing position. His head barely stuffed her cunt, which offered both erotic anticipation and aching frustration.

"What do you want, Rhiannon?"

"You."

She quivered. Her fingernails curled into the belt as she

imagined someone walking down the slight slope. He would spot them and stop, his gaze roving her exposed ass. He would see Jake's cock penetrating her and hear the slap of flesh against flesh. He would watch. And she would get off on it.

Jake pushed a little farther inside her and she whimpered.

He chuckled. "What do you want, Rhiannon?"

Her heart pounded and her body writhed in fervid heat. She moaned again, trying to work his cock farther inside her.

"Tell me what you want!" Jake demanded.

"I want you to fuck me," she roared in frustration. "Fuck me now, you prick!"

Jake thrust deeply and ended their mutual torment.

Pleasure pulsed in her swollen pussy. She gasped and groaned, frantically meeting Jake's every rough plunge.

He smacked her ass.

"Oh!" She was so startled, she lost their rhythm. She was surprised at how good the slap felt. The stinging pain reverberated straight to her pussy. "Again!"

He gave her another open-palm smack.

"Oh, God!" She went over the edge.

As pleasure cascaded in endlessly, she felt Jake's fingers dig into her skin. He pulled out, releasing her as his seed spattered the beach.

Rhiannon sank to her knees, gulping in air. Her wrists hurt and her ass throbbed, but she felt really, really good.

After Jake cleaned himself off and pulled up his pants, he untied her from the tree. She took off her thong and tucked it into her handbag. For a long moment, Jake hugged her as they regained their breath and their heartbeats slowed down.

"Thank you," she murmured against his throat. "Thank you for giving me the fantasy."

"My pleasure."

Rhiannon didn't know why she felt disappointed. Jake had given her lots of mind-blowing sex. She had saved up for this vacation so she could get her world royally rocked and that goal had been accomplished and then some.

Fantasyland was not the place to find a relationship.

Still, her heart broke just a little.

"Come back to my hotel room," he said. "I want to fall asleep with you. I want to wake up with you. I'll feed you pancakes and strawberries."

"My flight leaves in the morning. I have to take the early boat to the Bahamas."

"Stay longer."

"I can't, Jake. I have to go back to work and back to reality."

"Okay," he said, kissing her lightly. "I understand."

As Rhiannon settled into her coach seat, on the aisle no less, she sighed heavily. Jake hadn't asked her for phone number. He hadn't even called her hotel room to say good-bye.

It's just sex, Rhiannon. Get over it, girl. You had a great time with him and that's all you'll ever get.

Her pep talk depressed her even more. Had she believed there was a connection with Jake because she wanted one? Or had she fallen for another guy who had smooth lines, but no conscience?

"Excuse me, Miss Nelson?"

Rhiannon blinked up at the flight attendant. She was blond, perfectly made-up, and thin. "Yes?"

"I'm sorry, ma'am. Your seat has been reassigned. Will you come with me?"

Well, hell. She was already at the back of the plane. Where else were they going to put her? In the bathroom? She grabbed her purse and followed the tiny blonde down the narrow aisle.

The flight attendant took her to the first-class cabin and gestured to a window seat. The seat was huge and plush. Rhiannon looked at the chair, then at the blonde. "There must be some mistake."

"No, ma'am. You were upgraded to first class. Seat one-B is yours."

Rhiannon shrugged and sat down. Any minute now, someone would correct this error and she would be shuffled to the back of the plane. Oh, man, this seat was nice. Her ass actually fit in it and she had leg room.

"Champagne?"

She accepted the flute from a dark-haired flight attendant.

She figured she had better drink up while the getting was good. Her thoughts drifted back to Jake.

She stared out the circular window and sipped the champagne. She was so bummed out and so caught up in her yearning for someone she couldn't have that she didn't even turn to see who sat in the seat next to her.

"Champagne, sir?"

Rhiannon turned and gaped.

Jake sat next to her.

"Hi," he said.

The flute threatened to tilt, but he managed to pry her fingers off it and set the glass on the console between the seats.

"Jake! What are you doing here?"

"Did I mention my brother, Mike, is an airline pilot? He hooked me up with these seats."

Rhiannon stared at him, unable to formulate a sentence.

"You said I should see Reno."

She blinked. "You're leaving Fantasyland to go to Reno? It's a great city, but it doesn't have the same perks."

"But it has you," said Jake. He cupped her face and brushed his lips across hers. "And you're all the fantasy I need."

The Pirate's Pursuit

Pirate Island

Ahoy, matey! Welcome to Pirate Island! Though this island is the smallest in the Fantasyland Resort chain, you'll find it packed with pleasurable experiences—from luxury treatments at our day spas to gourmet dinners at our five-star restaurants.

We offer many enjoyable activities! Take a starlit sailing trip around Treasure Cove in a replica pirate sloop. Enjoy an evening of dancing with pirates and wenches at the Doubloon Saloon. Or take your pieces of eight and try your luck at the tables in our Gamblers' Lair.

Our most popular event for our female guests happens every night on Buccaneer's Beach: the Pirate's Pursuit. Dress up in your favorite costume—tavern wench, lady pirate, or noblewoman—and try to escape our lusty swashbucklers. Women are literally swept off their feet and spirited away for an evening of decadence.

We promise that your experiences on Pirate Island will shiver your timbers!

One
·······

"This is Janey's idea of research?" asked Lissa McClaskey as she examined the lobby of the Port Royal Inn.

Made to look like the innards of a pirate vessel, the walls were ribbed dark wood, polished to a high shine. Hanging big and bright above them was a chandelier—something not usually found in the bowels of a swashbuckler's ship. Neither were the white marble floors, the cozy arrangements of leather sofas and chairs, and the abundance of potted palms. Still, she had to admit the ambience was very piratelike.

Her temporary assistant, Sam Tremont, grinned boyishly. He was her younger sister's best friend. Her sis had developed a bad cold and copped out on the trip *she* had booked.

Janey had been her assistant since they played secretary and famous writer (Lissa's favorite game) as kids. Janey had been a precocious four-year-old and Lissa a very serious thirteen-year-old.

"Take Sam," Janey had sniffled via phone. "He knows everything I know and he's in between gigs."

Sam was a musician. He played guitar and sang beautifully. Lissa always wondered why Sam and Janey just didn't date and get it over with.

Almost ten years younger than Lissa, Sam was tall and lean and cute. He had wavy blond hair and green eyes that blinked owlishly out at her from behind horn-rimmed spectacles. If he lost his glasses and his penchant for khakis and dress shirts he never tucked in, he could . . . be mistaken for a surfer.

Instead he looked studious, which he was, and absentminded, which he wasn't.

"You wanted to experience the Golden Age of piracy. This place is as close as you're going to get." He heaved his laptop bag over his shoulder, gripping his suitcase in one hand and hers in the other. "Let's check in."

Lissa held her own laptop and her makeup case. Following her enthusiastic charge to the counter, she sighed. Sometimes, Sam was like a big puppy. She could hardly remember having the exuberance that seemed part and parcel of those still enjoying their twenties. Or maybe it was just Sam who never seemed to tire. She had discovered that there was no fact he couldn't unearth, no request he couldn't make happen, and no task he couldn't do.

Fantasyland

The only person who made a better assistant was Janey. Lissa depended on her sister absolutely. Janey made her life as an author bearable, shouldering all the necessary but unpleasant tasks that took away from Lissa's writing time. Lissa no longer dreaded book tours because Janey was there: her support, her friend, her conscience.

"It's a two-bedroom suite," said Sam, breaking into her thoughts. "Top floor, ocean view. Is that okay?"

"Yeah," said Lissa. "You said there's a real pirate's cove here?"

"I've already rented the schooner," he said, smiling. "The captain will take us to all the hot spots, including the cove. There's also a shipwreck in shallow water that we can scuba-dive through."

Lissa stared at his lips. He had a wonderful mouth. Oh! Her cheeks heated at the inappropriate direction of her thoughts. Sam was like her little brother and she'd been having not so sisterly thoughts about him. Lately, her libido had been . . . well, kinda frisky.

"Lissa?"

"Uh, yeah. Yeah, that's great."

Embarrassed, she turned away. The clerk handed over her credit card and said, "Let us know if you need anything else, Ms. McClaskey. It's our pleasure to serve you."

"Thanks."

Lissa and Sam headed toward the bank of elevators on the right side of the check-in counter.

"Is everything okay?" asked Sam.

Lissa worked up a smile and met his gaze. God, he was adorable. "Everything's terrific."

"Let me guess. You're suffering from Jack Sparrow syndrome."

Lissa looked up from her glass of seven and seven. The blond bartender, whose nametag read Wench Wendy, leaned on the polished wood bar and smiled. It was five o'clock in the evening, too late for afternoon libations and too early for dinner drinks. The hotel bar, called Kidd's Kavern, was practically empty.

"Jack Sparrow? From *Pirates of the Caribbean?*" Lissa grinned. That was one of her all-time favorite movies. In fact, she loved any story that put pirates in a romantic light. She knew from her research that pirates were bloodthirsty and ruthless, but they also knew how to have a good time.

"We get a lot of ladies who want to get swept off their feet by Johnny Depp." Wendy laughed.

"Don't I know it?" Lissa tapped the edge of her glass. "Can I have another one?"

Wendy poured Crown Royal into a glass and added a shot of 7-Up. After she slid the drink to Lissa, she grabbed a towel and started buffing the bar. "So what do you do?"

"I write historical romance novels," said Lissa. "You ever hear of the Pirate Prince series?"

Wendy shook her head. "Sorry. I get all the pirates I can take here. I'm into biographies and true crime books."

"Oh." Lissa traced the rim of her glass. "I write about pirates because I like the fantasy of getting captured and seduced by a seafaring rogue."

"You're in the right place then."

Another couple sat at the bar a few stools down from Lissa. Wendy walked away to tend to the new customers.

After Lissa had submitted her fifth Pirate Prince novel, her editor suggested she should consider writing a different kind of story. *How about a paranormal?* her editor had enthused during their last phone conversation. *Could you put a vampire in it?*

Lissa wanted to write a paranormal about as much as she wanted to endure a double root canal. But she was also a writer who knew on which side her bread was buttered, so she had roughed out a few ideas.

Luckily, her editor had gone for a vampire pirate pillaging on the high seas. If it meant getting to write another historical and keeping her Pirate Prince series alive, she'd put in as many preternatural creatures as her publisher wanted. Sure, Lissa had a few logistics to figure out. Where did a vampire captain sleep during the day? What kind of crew would tolerate an undead leader? How did they pillage anything or anyone at night?

Lissa drained the rest of her drink. Where was Sam? After they'd gotten settled into the suite, she'd taken a nap, and when she awoke, she found a note from him asking for her to meet him at this bar.

"Miss McClaskey?"

She looked up at Wendy. The woman handed her a single white rose and vellum envelope. It had a wax seal on it. Weird.

"What's this?"

"Just arrived, ma'am. I was told to give it to you."

Curious, Lissa popped off the seal and slid out the single sheet of paper.

> *A pirate on a quest*
> *To find a maiden true*
> *Honor this humble behest*
> *And let him capture you. . . .*

Below the odd poem were two words: *Treasure Trove.*

Lissa frowned at the handwriting. She didn't recognize the sweeping broad strokes. Who the hell would send her an invitation to be shanghaied?

"What do you make of this?" asked Lissa, handing the page to Wendy.

The bartender's gaze flicked over the words and she grinned. "You've been invited to the Pirate's Pursuit. Pirates row onto Buccaneer's Beach and chase their ladies."

"What happens if the pirate catches you?"

"Whatever you want."

Lissa's brows rose. What the hell had Janey booked them into? Sure, there were plenty of pirate activities here, but it seemed most guests were living out fantasies of a more sensual nature. Not that Lissa was opposed to such a thing. She frowned. She couldn't remember the last time she'd had sex. How sad was that?

She untucked her cell phone from its slot on the side of her purse and dialed Sam.

"Hello?"

"I'm at Kidd's Kavern. Where are you?"

"Sorry, boss. I'm stuck in the business office. Fax machine is giving me fits."

"Fax?"

"The galleys, remember?"

She'd corrected the last of them on the plane to the Bahamas. On the boat ride to this island, she'd given those pages to Sam. She didn't have to tell him what to do—he just did it. The boy never let the grass grow under his feet.

"I'm going to take the night off," Lissa said. "Why don't you, too? Go find yourself a hottie to dance the night away with."

She blanched. She didn't really want the idea of Sam's arms around some hot, young thing galloping through her mind, but there it was, depressingly vivid. Yep. She'd be cute, tan, and thin, and she'd giggle adorably.

Blech.

Sam was silent for a long moment. Then he said, "Who

are you? And what have you done with my lovable worka-holic?"

"Ha. Ha. *Ha*." Lissa looked at the invitation. Was she nuts? She didn't know who had sent her this note. Still, she couldn't give up an opportunity to get chased by a pi-rate. Jack Sparrow syndrome, all right. She'd just let him capture her, then call it a night.

That sounded reasonable. Play a little, harmless game, then go back to the suite for room service and a thousand words on the new manuscript.

"Lissa?"

"Sorry, I zoned out there. Finish wrestling that fax ma-chine into submission and go have some fun. That's an order."

"Yes, ma'am."

She hung up, plucked her rose and invite from the bar, then laid down a twenty. After waving good-bye to Wendy, she left Kidd's Kavern and crossed the lobby to the con-cierge's desk.

"Yes, ma'am?" asked a thin man with graying hair. He was dressed in a stylish black suit. It was probably too much to ask a concierge to wear an eye patch and sword and inter-sperse conversations with "Yarr!"

"When is the Pirate's Pursuit?"

"Tonight's game begins at seven p.m."

Lissa glanced at the paper again. "Do you know what the Treasure Trove is?"

"The shop is located in our mall. You go down the hallway until you reach the staircase. Go up the stairs, and through the door is the first floor of our shopping center. The Treasure Trove is the third storefront on the left."

"Thanks."

Ten minutes later, Lissa entered the Treasure Trove. The small shop had paneled walls, red carpet, and low lighting. The store was filled with racks and racks of clothes and many shelves of hats, shoes, and accessories.

"'Ello, luv," said a large woman with brassy red hair and sparkling green eyes. Her name tag read GENESSA. She was dressed like a gypsy, in layers of purple and white, her bell-laden belt jangling as she rounded the counter. "What can I do for you?"

"I was invited to the Pirate's Pursuit." Lissa's cheeks heated as she said the words. Oh, for heaven's sake! Why was she embarrassed about indulging in an innocuous fantasy? She'd consider it research. Yeah. *Research.*

"What's your name, luv?" Her cockney accent was thick.

"Lissa McClaskey."

Genessa reached into a rack of plastic-covered clothes and plucked out a dress. "Oh-ho. This here's a good 'un. Your pirate likes his girls lusty."

Lissa accepted the costume. "What do I owe you?"

"It's been paid for, miss. All you need to do is wear it. Be sure you put on the colored sash—that's how your pirate will identify you."

Well, shiver me timbers.

Two
· · · · · · · ·

L issa sat on the couch in her hotel suite and stared at the costume draped next to her. Now that she'd had time to think about her impulse, she was chickening out.

The last man she'd dated was Ian. That was . . . God, three years ago. He was a successful architect who was handsome, ambitious, and charming. Everyone had their faults, but Ian's main flaw had been his obsession with his job.

Lissa understood something about obsession—after all, she was a writer, and she often immersed herself in a fictional world to the point where she eschewed showers, ate cereal for dinner, and lived in the same pair of sweats for a week.

But Ian had needed a woman more interested in him and his career and Lissa had wanted a man who wasn't a self-absorbed prick.

They'd parted ways. And she hadn't had a serious relationship since then. Oh, the occasional date, but nothing that had led to hot sex, much less a long-term relationship. In fact, the only man currently in her life was Sam.

Sam was a nice kid. Cute. Really cute. Smart. Funny. *What are you doing, Lissa?* Sam, for all intents and purposes belonged to Janey. He was not a boy toy. She sighed.

According to Lissa's mother, compatibility was *the* most important quality in a relationship. Mom had told her numerous times that the first bright passion associated with falling in love faded with time. *You find someone you can like for the rest of your life,* she said. *Sex is nice, honey, but decent conversation and a faithful heart are worth a lot more.*

Of course, her mother had been married four times in the hopes of finding a man who didn't bore her to tears or cheat on her. So far, she hadn't found him.

Lissa needed to stop thinking that life was like a romance novel. People didn't fall in love in a day and stay madly in love for the rest of their lives. Passion burned bright and quick before it flickered out.

Well, hell. Lissa stood up and plucked the dress off the couch. Maybe a relationship was too much to hope for, but fun—well, that she could have without worrying about things like compatibility.

Dressed as a tavern wench, Lissa walked barefoot on the beach. The knee-length skirt showed off her legs. The red sash cinched her waist; she'd knotted it on the side so that the ends would flow off her hip.

The white shirt puffed at the shoulders, leaving her arms bare. With help from her strapless push-up bra, the low-cut blouse gave new meaning to the word "cleavage." Bangles clinked on her wrists. On her left ankle she'd put a bell-filled bracelet. She'd taken her time getting ready, soaking in a lavender-scented bath and patting her entire body with a sparkly, scented powder. She kept her makeup light and left her brown hair long and straight.

Rows of bamboo torches offered the only light on the dark beach. Stars glittered like diamonds in the night sky. As Lissa walked toward the water, a warm breeze teased the edge of her skirt and tossed her hair. The low waves licked at her toes and she curled them into the sand, enjoying the sensation of the soft grit tickling her feet.

She scanned the ocean, enjoying its dark, shining beauty. In the distance, she spotted a large row boat headed toward the shore. Loud singing floated toward her: "Yo-ho, yo-ho, a pirate's life for me!"

Her heart turned over in her chest and adrenaline hummed up her spine. The boat hit the shore and men tumbled out of the craft, laughing and singing.

"We come for ye, wenches!" cried one.

The pirates swarmed the beach, brandishing swords and whooping loudly. Women giggled and screamed as they ran every which way.

One pirate swaggered toward Lissa. He wore a red hand-kerchief over his hair and a red mask that covered half his face. His teeth were bared in a lascivious grin. Wow. His loose shirt offered tantalizing glimpses of muscled flesh. As he passed by a torch, the flickering light revealed a chiseled pro-file.

"Lissa! I'll show ye a good time!" he crowed in a gravelly voice.

Her heart tripled its frantic beat. Oh, God. This was him. The pirate who wanted her! She sucked in a steadying breath. *Time to put up or shut up, girl.*

His arms opened wide. "Are ye gonna embrace me, ye bonny lass?"

She'd written enough pirate dialogue to know how to respond. "I wouldn't let a scurvy dog like you anywhere near my goods," she said saucily, as she tossed her hair over her shoulder.

His eyes flashed with surprise. He paused in the dark space between two torches, so his expression was hidden, but obviously he was calculating the distance between them.

He shot toward her.

Lissa turned and ran. Adrenaline spiked in her belly as he gave chase. She worked out three days a week; she had the stamina needed to make her pirate work for his bounty. Even so, she didn't want to run too hard or too long.

She didn't need to worry. In mere moments, she felt him

close behind her. She heard his boots dig into the sand and his breath draw in as he lunged for her. His arms snaked around her waist and he pulled her snug against him.

"Hey!" she yelled, flailing her arms and legs.

He laughed. "Scurvy dog, am I?"

Panic clawed at her, even though she knew this was just a game. What had she been thinking? She didn't know this man. How could she trust him? Was she really going to let a stranger whisk her away? Was she this desperate to find a human connection, to get a few moments of plea-sure?

"Sshh, now, lass. I won't hurt ye."

Whoa. Her pirate had sensed her distress. She gulped in air and tried to calm down. Her heart felt like it was going to beat out of her chest.

"This is your game," the pirate whispered in a normal voice. "You end it whenever you want, just say the word."

Slowly, the pirate released her. He still held her flush against his body, but her feet sank reassuringly into the sand. He leaned down and whispered, "What's it to be, lass? Are ye with me? Or do I find a more willing wench?"

Lissa drew in a steadying breath. "You caught me fair and square. I'm yours."

His low chuckle made her tingle. His fingers drifted up her arms and she shivered. "And I'm yours, lass. Now I will make off with ye to my secret cave. Ye cannot know the way, so I must blindfold you."

"O-okay."

A red cloth appeared over her shoulder and her pirate drew it across her throat, over her face, and finally, around the top of her head. She closed her eyes as he tied material.

"Are ye ready?"

She nodded. Delicious tension wound through her. Taken to a pirate's cave for ravishing!

He scooped her up and she yelped, throwing her arms around his shoulders.

"Snuggle in, lass," he said. "It's a bit of a walk."

Getting toted around like a precious treasure was a new experience, and one that she enjoyed. She did exactly as he asked: She snuggled into his embrace. God, he smelled good. He was all hard muscle and sinewy strength. As he proceeded toward their unknown destination, Lissa smiled.

Lissa's pirate laid her gently on a soft surface.

"Where are we?" she asked as she raised her hands to undo the band's knot.

"You're safe." His hands stilled hers. "Leave it for a moment, lass."

"Okay." She realized that he was standing in front of her. Her stomach felt as if it were filled with frantic butterflies. She pressed a palm against her belly. "What now?"

"We can talk. Or I can feed you."

"Feed me?" She licked her lips. "Like that scene in *Nine and a Half Weeks*?"

His low, sexy chuckle made her tummy butterflies do the mambo. "Aye. We have strawberries."

How brave was she? Could she dive fully into the fantasy of being a pirate's captive? Just for tonight, she could be a saucy wench.

"I'm nervous," she admitted.

"That's all right, lass," said the pirate. "It's a game. When you want to stop, you say so."

"Should we at least exchange names?"

"If ye like."

"I'm Lissa."

She felt the bed give way as he sat next to her. She could feel him very near, but not quite close enough that he was touching her.

"Ye can call me Edward."

"Edward Teach?" she asked, laughing. "I'm in the presence of Blackbeard."

"I'm more handsome than that rogue," he scoffed. She felt the light scrape of his fingertips on her arm. "You're very pretty."

"Thank you."

His fingers coasted over her shoulder and grazed her neck. He brushed back her hair, combing his fingers through the strands.

"Ye hair is like silk." As his fingers sifted her well-brushed tresses, she felt him lean forward. His hot breath ghosted over her neck. "Hmm. Ye smell good, too."

With each touch, her heart beat faster and her belly squeezed. It had been too long since anyone had made her tingle with anticipation. She found it discombobulating that this stranger could stoke her into the kind of sensual heat that she always wrote about but rarely experienced.

When Edward's lips dropped on the rapid pulse at the base of her throat, she sucked in a startled breath.

"Do ye want me to stop?" he asked softly.

The words tickled her skin. She couldn't articulate a response, so she reached for him and dragged her fingers through his soft hair. She pressed his skull lightly to let him know she wanted him to stay. He had taken off the mask and the handkerchief covering his head, too.

His lips traveled up her neck, resting on the spot just below her earlobe. His tongue flicked her skin, snaking up to tease the shell of her ear. Her breath quickened as desire sparked all the way through her.

"Ye are a fine morsel. One I would gladly devour." He lifted away from her. In a regular voice, he whispered, "I have to know how far you want to go, Lissa. Do you want me to kiss you, feed you strawberries, and let you go? Do you want me tie you up and ravage you while you protest? Tell me what you want."

"And you'll give it to me?"

"This is Fantasyland. My whole purpose is to indulge your every desire."

Lissa's heart skipped a beat.

He shuddered, then sighed. His head dropped to her shoulder. "I want to kiss you," he admitted in a ragged voice. "Everywhere. I want to kiss you and I don't want to stop."

Lissa shivered at his confession. "I would like that."

"I'll give ye a choice, lass. Ye can let me seduce you with the blindfold on or . . ."

His pause went on for a beat too long.

"Or what?"

"Ye can choose to know who I am."

Three

L issa swallowed the knot in her throat. Had Janey hired someone at the resort to sweep her off her feet? Could she look into the eyes of a complete stranger and still go through with the seduction?

Or should she pretend to be the reluctantly ravaged wench? This man would be her pirate prince and she would be his captive. Her belly quivered at the very idea. She could experience wanton pleasure. For once in her life, she could be the star in her very own romance.

"Better I know not who you are," she said haughtily, "lest I inform the authorities of your identity."

"Oh-ho, you dare threaten me, wench?" He grasped her arm and pulled her off the bed. "Then I better make sure you don't escape."

He led her to another part of the room. She felt something wide and soft wrapped around each of her wrists. He lifted her arms above her head and hooked them to what she assumed was an attachment hanging from the ceiling.

"You're mine."

Lissa trembled at the possessiveness infused into those two words.

"Say it," demanded her pirate. "Say that you're mine."

"No," she cried. Her heart trilled as she dove completely into their game. "Never!"

"I'll make you say it," he promised darkly. "I'll make you beg for me."

She felt his hand curl into the middle of her bodice. His fingers brushed the tops of her breasts, causing a riot of sensations that danced all the way to her pussy.

Then he yanked her bodice down.

The shirt ripped in half easily and fell open, revealing her breasts, clasped in the silky white bra. She heard the sharp intake of his breath and suspected he was studying her boobs. Too bad she was blindfolded. She wanted to see his lusty glances. At least, she hoped his glances were lusty.

He stepped close to her, his body pressed enticingly against hers. His lips brushed her ear.

"If you want to stop playing, then say 'Roses are red.' If I hear that phrase, I'll stop everything and let you go. Do you understand?"

She nodded.

His knuckles caressed the side of her neck. "You are beautiful. So very, very beautiful."

"You are a rogue. A blackguard!" She nearly giggled. She never thought she'd have the opportunity to call someone a "blackguard." She pretended to struggle and the chains above her rattled.

"Don't forget my promise, wench. You will beg for my touch." He laughed softly. "And you *will* tell me that you're mine."

He walked away, leaving her to ponder his words and to wonder what he might be doing. She heard paper rattles, cloth whispers, and metal clinks.

She felt his return, though he didn't touch her. It was his presence that surrounded her, that made her heart pound faster. His lips descended, peppering the tops of her breasts. The tender ravishment made her tremble. Reaching around, he unhooked her bra. Since it was strapless, the undergarment fell away easily.

Whoa. Blindfolded, chained, and exposed from the waist up—a girl couldn't get more vulnerable than that. She ached to feel his lips again. He cupped her breasts, thumbs brushing her nipples. The light touches felt wonderful, but she didn't want to appear as if she were caving in to his seduction.

Well, not yet.

He gripped her nipple between his fingers, squeezing lightly. Pleasure weaved through her and she swallowed her moan. God, it had been so long since she'd felt this way.

"Do you relent?" he murmured.

"Never."

"Then I must torture you until you beg for mercy."

Something long and metal slid over her skin, clamping the base of the tight peak. A second clamp claimed her other nipple. Delectable tendrils of pain throbbed in her breasts.

Lissa shivered.

"This chain is attached to another, longer chain." He tugged on the fetter.

Sensual agony shot through her breasts, zapping the pit of her stomach before settling heavy and hot in her pussy. For a moment, her thoughts scattered and all she could process was her body's enthrallment.

His hands coasted down her stomach and brought her mind back into focus. Oh, hell. Was he going to rip her skirt, too? Instead of tearing apart another piece of clothing, he inched the material off her hips. After taking off the skirt, he rubbed her thighs, her calves, and even her feet. He jiggled the bell ankle bracelet and chuckled.

Her underwear went next.

Except for the ripped shirt that still hung from her shoulders, she was naked. Doubts crept through her passion. Was this the right thing to do? Was playing a game with a stranger really fulfilling a fantasy?

She was almost positive Janey set up this situation. If that were the case, her sister would never put her in a situation that wasn't safe. However, Janey and she were going to have a long talk about booking research trips at sex resorts.

Her pirate stayed in the kneeling position. She knew this because she felt his lips ghost along her left hip. Her lungs stalled and her heart hammered.

As his tongue slid between her moist pussy lips, he pulled on the chain.

The shock of pain stole her breath. A moan warbled from her throat.

"You like it," he accused. "Don't you, my captive?"

"I do *not*. You're torturing an innocent woman."

"No woman is innocent—especially not you." He pierced her slick entrance with two fingers. "Here is the evidence of your lies."

He withdrew his fingers and used them to part her labia. The chain bounced against her stomach as he lifted the loose end. Then . . . oh then . . . he clamped her clitoris. The pressure was intense, but not unbearable. Her whole body tingled with pleasure-pain.

He started licking her tortured clit. He built and stoked a sensual fire that burned brighter and hotter with every flick of his tongue.

Her pussy throbbed, her clit tightened with pleasure, and streamers of bliss threatened.

Then the bastard abandoned her.

She couldn't stop the cry of frustration.

"There's a way to end your torment." He circled around her. She felt the steel warmth of his body—his very nude body—pressed against her. His penis slid between her buttocks. Oh, God. "Just answer one question."

He lifted her hair and feathered kisses on her neck. Then his hands drifted down to her thighs, trailing up her ribs oh so slowly until his hands cupped her breasts. He squeezed. Sensations rolled down to her tormented pussy.

"Do your worst, pirate. I am stronger than you believe."

His fingers tangled in the chain looped between her nipples. He tugged it.

Pain erupted from her nipples. The sensations overwhelmed her as agony morphed into pleasure. The intensity was incredible. God in heaven! She'd never felt anything like this before.

How much more could she take?

"Who do you belong to?" he asked. He released her breasts and slid his palms down to her hips. He took the chain attached to her clitoris and fingered it.

A moan escaped. Then her throat knotted and she swallowed the answer he wanted to hear.

"Tell me," he whispered.

She sucked in a breath. Sweat beaded on her skin, her arms were started to ache, and her body felt as though it had been set on fire.

But she wasn't yet ready to end this part of the game.

He pulled up on the chain. The clamp squeezing her clitoris shifted and the excruciating pain buckled her knees.

He held on to her. His breath was harsh against his neck. "Who do you belong to?"

The words seemed to soak into her skin. She leaned against him, taking in his strength because she had none of her own. Her whole body hummed in sexual expectation.

"You," she uttered, defeated. "I belong to you."

He reached up and took her wrists off the ceiling hook. Then he scooped her into his arms and carried her to the bed. The thick coverlet felt soft and comfortable. It was a definite contrast to her sensually tormented body, which still writhed with hot need.

He rolled her onto her side and spooned behind her. For a long moment, all she felt was the stroking of his hands on her sensitized skin. His sweet tending to her body only enflamed her more. She pressed against him, no longer in control of her actions. His cock pulsed against her ass and she wiggled, causing him to groan.

"Do you want something, my captive?"

"Fuck me!"

"Only if you beg."

He continued to rub her body, ignoring the areas she wanted him to touch the most: her aching breasts and her throbbing pussy.

"Please!" She was through with the game. She craved the relief only his cock offered. She wanted to feel his penetration. She wanted him to bring her to orgasm. "Please," she repeated. "Fuck me!"

"Get on your hands and knees, wench."

His voice was gruff and she realized he was on the edge himself. That little tidbit served to make her hotter.

She rolled onto her hands and knees and eagerly lifted her ass. He held on to her hips and worked his cock inside her wet heat. She nearly wept at the sense of relief that filled her when he pushed all the way inside. Vaguely, she realized he was wearing a condom, though she had no idea when he'd had the time to put it on.

After a few slow strokes, he created a steady rhythm. He pounded into her and she loved it. She cried for more, her words tangling in her moans.

His hand crept around her waist.

She was on fire now, excitement rippling. *OhGodoh-GodohGod* . . .

He jerked on the chain nearest her clit.

Her orgasm exploded.

She seemed to fly into the stars and she floated there, soaking in the light and heat until she plummeted to earth. Her pirate tensed and plunged deeply. His fingers dug into her hips as he ejaculated. He didn't move or breathe for what seemed forever.

Lissa collapsed on the bed. He withdrew and pressed a kiss on each of her buttocks. She laughed as he scooted off the bed, presumably to dispose of the condom.

Oh, Lord. That was the most fun she'd had in a really, really long time. Her thoughts wandered to Sam. What was he doing? Had he found himself a hot, young thing?

Her pirate hadn't returned, but she was ready to see him. She dragged off the blindfold. God, her makeup was probably in shambles.

She swung her legs off the round bed. She blinked. Wow. They really were in a cave. The small, dark room held the bed, with its red velvet bedspread and heart-shaped pillows, a table laden with fruit, chocolate truffles, hors d'oeuvres, and champagne. Lit votive candles in wall sconces and tapers in the chandelier offered low, flickering light.

Though bordering on cheesy, the room was still romantic.

Lissa heard a noise and she looked up into the startled gaze of her pirate. Oh, no. No!

Her heart dropped to her toes. *Oh. My. God.* "Please . . . please . . . do not tell me that I just slept with *you.*"

Four
·········

S am smiled. "I'd say we did a little more than plain ol' sleeping together. Do you need help taking off the Y clamps?"

Lissa looked down and realized how incredibly naked she was. Naked and chained up like a pirate's whore. *Janey is gonna kill me.*

She pulled at a nipple clamp and pain shot through her. Damn it.

"You can't just yank them off," he said.

He was naked, too. And he was freaking gorgeous. He was muscled, and he looked so unlike studious Sam or even musician Sam, she couldn't quite comprehend that this man was . . . was . . . her sister's perfect man.

He leaned down to unclip one of her nipples and she yelped, rearing back. "Don't touch me!"

"I've already touched you. And I have every intention of touching you again."

"No," said Lissa, horrified. "This is so wrong. Janey—"

"Thinks you're thickheaded. She also thinks that you and I are perfect for each other."

This information stalled Lissa's retreat. She blinked at Sam as he crawled on the bed toward her. "S-she does?"

He pried open her legs and gently released the clamp on her clitoris. He kissed her tingling nub, flicking his tongue on the tortured flesh.

"Don't!" Lissa said.

He looked at her and grinned. "You're still my captive."

"Sam, I'm way older than you."

"Only by nine years and three months." His gaze twinkled. "You act like you're older than Methuselah. You're only thirty-three."

"And you're twenty-four. I'm robbing the cradle."

"I'm not a child. Do you need me to prove it again?"

"You need to date Janey."

"Janey and I are friends. That's all we've ever been, Lissa."

Had her pirate been anyone other than Sam, she would enjoy a night spent here in his brawny arms. Actually, she'd already let him ravish her. What was the point of denying that they'd had fantastic sex?

He grabbed her legs and pulled her down. He lay beside her, taking the clamps off her nipples. He kissed the abused flesh and she let him do it because, well, it felt wonderful.

"Remember Thanksgiving?" he asked.

Sam had joined her crazy family for Turkey Day. He'd gone outside to play with the kids instead of opting for an afternoon of watching football. Lissa, as the oldest McClaskey sibling, not to mention childless and husbandless, had babysitting duty. She'd watched Sam almost more than she'd watched the kids.

It was no coincidence that her "frisky" libido had kicked in about that time. Though she denied it then, she'd felt the attraction between them. She felt comfortable with him and he made her laugh. He was a good listener, too. It was rare to find a man genuinely interested in what she had to say.

Sam unchained her wrist and then kissed her pulse. "I thought I finally had you. I've been waiting for the day you didn't look at me like I was a little boy."

"Sam . . ."

"You said you were mine."

"That was a game. I didn't know who you were."

His lips thinned and his eyes flashed with pain. "So you would hand over your body to a stranger, but not to someone who loves you?"

"You love me?"

Her heart pounded fiercely. This was getting way out of hand. Sex was one thing. Love was something else.

Lissa nibbled her lower lip. She should lie to him. She should say he was a nice guy but not the one for her. Why give him hope?

Maybe it was that she didn't want to give herself hope.

"You want to stay, don't you?"

Lissa nodded. "This is wrong," she whispered. "I don't want you to get hurt."

He kissed her lightly. The brief contact had the power to make her tremble.

"I love you. I'm not sorry I told you, either. I get it, Lissa. You don't know what to think, what to say. What we've started tonight can last for longer than just a weekend at Fantasyland. I'll give you all the time and space you need, but I won't give up."

"You're saying that I'll never be rid of you." She nearly laughed. He was so serious. How could he know, at the tender age of twenty-four, what he wanted? Or *who* he wanted? She was thirty-three and she still didn't know what the hell she wanted from life or from love.

"Damn right. You're mine and I'm yours."

Lissa gave in. She wanted Sam. Lust was simple. But he wanted more from her than just sex. If she let herself, she might let herself fall in love with him, too.

But tonight . . . tonight was about the fantasy.

She pushed him onto his back and crawled between his legs. He had given her such exquisite pleasure that she wanted to give him the same. They had all night to play.

Now it was Sam's turned to be tortured.

Lissa turned onto her side. Leaning forward, she kissed his naked chest. His skin was all muscled curves and ridges.

She feasted on his pectorals, kissing every centimeter of flesh. She laved his tiny brown nipples into hardness, then flicked her tongue across each nub.

He groaned and the sound rumbled in his mouth.

She licked the space between his pecs, tasting the faint musk of his skin. As she explored his body with fingers and lips, his hands were restless on her back, her shoulders, her buttocks.

Her engine was getting revved up all over again. Sam looped his hands under her arms and pulled her forward so his mouth could ravage her breasts.

Zings traveled from nipples to pussy as he tugged one peak, then the other, between his teeth and flicked his tongue rapidly against the turgid points. The need built—an ache that bloomed between her thighs.

Despite his protests, she scooted down and rubbed her nipples over his chest. She reached between their bodies and grasped his hard-on. She squeezed his cock, then caressed it. Yummy. She adored the feel of his shaft against her palm.

"Let me taste you," she murmured.

She crawled between his legs, her hands coasting up his thighs. Lissa wanted to feel that big, thick cock slide inside her again. She fondled his balls, squeezing them lightly. Sam's hands fisted in the bedcovers and his hips thrust, a silent begging for her mouth. She ignored that plea, stroking him roughly, then softly.

Finally Lissa took his cock into her mouth and sucked on

it, working his length into full hardness. She enjoyed the taste of his maleness, loved how his shaft slid between her willing lips.

She savored his cock, kissing it from base to head before taking the tip into her mouth and sucking it. Torturing him with endless tongue swirls and long licks, she took all of him.

His hands dove into her hair and held her captive. Not content with her gentle worshipping, he fucked her mouth. She held on to his thighs and took his strokes, her tongue teasing the cock pumping between her lips.

With a persecuted groan, Sam released her, gasping and panting. She saw precome pearl on the tip of his penis and she sucked it away.

Sam looked at her, his eyes glazed. "I want you."

"I'll fuck you," she said, "but don't come."

"You don't ask for much, do you?"

Smiling wickedly, she rose to her knees, then planted herself on either side of his hips. She slid her hand between her legs and pinched her clit. Preorgasm shivers racked her. She rubbed her slick inner folds, then spread them apart and showed him her cunt.

"Oh, God."

"Just remember, you started it." Lissa pressed down and slicked her pussy across his cock.

Reaching down, Lissa guided Sam's cock inside her pussy.

Their breathing was harsh, shallow. Their gazes mirrored passion. Sam grasped her hips and thrust upward. His calculated strokes drove her mad. An ache stole across her, made her belly tight with need, made her core spiral with pleasure.

He released her hips and played with her breasts, pulling on her sensitive nipples, bringing her closer and closer to orgasm.

Then she felt his thumb stroking her clit and she squeezed her vaginal muscles as she fucked him, over and over.

"Don't come," she warned him. "Not yet."

"You're . . . killing . . . me."

The bliss sparked and *wham!* She shattered into a thousand glittering shards.

"Lissa . . ."

She lifted off him and kneeled between his legs again. She licked her own essence off his cock. She enjoyed the taste of his maleness mixed with her quintessence, loved how his shaft slid between her willing lips.

His fingers pressed against her skull. His moans were low and harsh as she took his cock again and again. She gripped his thighs and increased her efforts. His cock was so hard, the veins bulged.

"I'm going to come, Lissa!"

She felt that first delicate tremble and sucked him to the base.

He came hard, his hot spunk splashing down her throat. She swallowed every drop as residual spasms caused his cock to pulse in the warm cave of her mouth.

She licked him clean, kissing his softening flesh.

When she sat up, she looked at him.

"That was incredible," he said. "C'mere."

Despite her better judgment, Lissa snuggled beside him. He wrapped his arms around her and kissed her temple. She felt so relaxed, so happy, so . . . loved.

Oh, hell. *What have I done?*

Five

Lissa awoke and blinked away the fog of sleep. She found herself nose to nose with Sam. He was awake, looking as cute as ever, and his hand was pressed against her pussy.

"What are you doing?" she asked sleepily. She smiled. "Do it some more."

He chuckled. "I want to wake up with you every morning. I want to make love to you every night."

"Hmm. That's a hell of an offer."

"But you're not going to take it, are you?"

"I'm getting used to this, to us." Lissa kissed him. "It scares me, how I feel about you."

"I know." He nuzzled her neck. His mouth dropped to her breasts and licked her nipples to hardness. "I want you, Lissa. Right now."

"I won't fight you, my gorgeous pirate. I'm yours, remember?"

"Do you trust me?"

"Yes."

Sam grinned. "Okay. Roll onto your stomach. I'll be right back."

Lissa did as he asked, wondering what he was up to now. She closed her eyes, feeling groggy, as she listened to him move around the room.

She almost launched off the bed when she felt his finger probe her anus.

"Relax," he murmured.

"Easy for you to say! What are you doing?"

"Trying to pleasure you."

A few seconds later, she felt something smaller pierce her anal opening. The cold squirt of lubricant filled her ass.

Her heart raced. She'd never had anal sex. Whoa. Was she ready for this?

Sam inserted his finger again and stretched her opening. Okay, that felt weird.

Then he put in another finger.

She sucked in startled breath. Jeez! The lubricant made the pressure tolerable, but when was the pleasure supposed to begin?

He continued to stretch her until she could comfortably take both fingers. "Perfect."

He removed his fingers and she sighed with relief. She

heard the squirt of the lubricant again and realized he was rubbing something else with the gel. Her stomach squeezed in dread even as her body reacted to the eroticism of trying something new, something forbidden.

He parted her buttocks and fitted something round and plastic against her pucker.

"Push back as I push in."

"What is it?"

"An anal plug. Trust me, you'll like it." The first part of the plug slid in without too much trouble, but the flared base caused a burning sensation.

"It's all the way in now. How does it feel?"

"Do you really want to know?"

He laughed.

He rolled her onto her side, then slid next to her. He played with her breasts, suckling her nipples as his hands stroked her body into carnal heat.

As Sam kissed and touched her, she fell under his sensual spell all over again. After a while, she realized her ass had adjusted to the fullness of the butt plug.

Sam rolled off the bed long enough to sheath his cock in a condom.

"Hold on to me, Lissa."

She gripped his shoulders as he lifted her leg and worked his cock deeper and deeper into her pussy. The sensations that radiated from her ass and pussy tormented her deliciously.

God! She couldn't believe how stuffed she felt. What shocked her most was that she liked the double penetration.

Sam fucked her with slow, deliberate movements. His gaze captured hers and wouldn't let go. One hand held on to her thigh. He was at the right angle to bump her clit.

Pleasure shuddered through her.

Then Sam reached down and pressed a button on the plug.

It started vibrating.

Euphoria sparked and built higher and higher. Sam's thrusts got faster, harder. And the plug in her ass shook her into an ecstasy she'd never believed possible.

Her orgasm imploded.

Sensation after sensation blazed from her cunt to every nerve in her body.

"Lissa!" Sam stilled, his cock pulsating inside her as he found his release.

They collapsed against each other.

"Is it always going to be so . . . so . . . amazing?" Lissa asked.

"Yes," said Sam. "Always."

"So when's the wedding?" asked Janey. Lissa and she were talking via cell phone.

"Ha. Ha." Lissa stood on the balcony of the suite and looked at the ocean. The afternoon sun glittered in a cloudless blue sky. This place truly was paradise. "I'm still getting used to being his girlfriend. One step at a time, okay?"

"Yeah, yeah." Janey sounded much, much better, the faker. She hadn't been sick at all. She'd booked the trip and manipulated the situation so that Sam would take the trip with Lissa.

Janey and Sam had planned the whole thing. Lissa was too happy to be really pissed off about it, but that didn't mean she wouldn't seek sisterly revenge at some point.

"Well, don't let me keep you," said Janey. "I know you have things . . . or cute guys named Sam . . . to do."

"Oh, you bet I do. You know, last night, he pulled out this ostrich feather. Then he—"

"Yuck! I do not want to hear the sexual details of my best friend and my sister's sex life."

"But you don't have one," Lissa pointed out. "So I thought I'd share mine."

"I'm hanging up, you cow. Love you."

Lissa laughed as she hung up the cell phone.

Sam came up behind her and wrapped his arms around her waist. "Janey okay?"

"Yeah. But you knew that, didn't you?"

He nuzzled her neck. "Maybe."

He untied her robe and the garment fell open.

"Sam! We're on a balcony in front of God and every-one."

"So what?" He edged the robe off her shoulders and let it fall to the concrete. He jostled her toward the balcony's railing. "Hold on to it."

Delicious shivers racked her body as she bent over and grabbed the railing.

She was learning that Sam was unafraid of trying anything. He'd given her more new experiences in bed than she'd had in her entire sexually active life.

She heard a tiny whir, and before she had a chance to voice the obvious question, Sam slid the lubricated vibrator into her pussy.

The implement had an extension that tickled her clitoris with every plunge of the fake cock. Her breasts swayed to the rhythm established by Sam. The vibrator brought her closer and closer to her peak.

She moaned, gripping the rail as she met every exquisite plunge of the vibrator.

"Oh, God! Sam, I'm going to come!"

She tipped over the edge, pleasure bursting from her core. The sensations wrapped around her as her pussy sucked at the still vibrating cock.

Sam wasn't finished with her.

"Stay here." He disappeared for scant moments. When he returned to the balcony, he pressed against her ass and slid his sheathed cock inside her weeping pussy.

He fucked her hard. Her battered pussy was still post-orgasmic, but she loved the feel of him thrusting inside her.

She kept one hand on the rail, but loosened the other so she could play with her breasts.

That was when Sam smacked her ass.

The shock of pain electrified her pussy. She moaned and alternated twisting her nipples. Her bliss built up in her quivering core.

He slapped her other buttock. She never would've believed herself capable of reacting erotically to a spanking, but Sam had taught her that she was very responsive to myriad sensations.

He whacked her again.

The pain radiated to her throbbing cunt and joined with the budding orgasm. Oh, God. Yes!

The next spanking sent her spiraling over the edge. Her joy bloomed fully and pleasure cascaded endlessly through her.

Sam cried out and shoved his cock so deep inside her, she felt him at the entrance to her womb. His cock shuddered inside her pussy as his fingers dug into her ass.

After a long moment of trying to breathe again, Sam withdrew and she stood up. He picked up the robe and clothed her in it.

She mixed up a batch of margaritas in their kitchenette while Sam cleaned up. He came into the living room wearing only a sexy grin. He certainly was more prince than pirate.

"To fantastic, awe-inspiring sex," she said, handing Sam his drink.

He clinked his glass to hers. "To true love."

Lissa wasn't sure if she and Sam were a forever kind of love. Oh, what the hell? Janey had probably already planned the wedding anyway.

"To true love," she said. And smiled.

Isle of Dark Delights

The Isle of Dark Delights caters to guests who enjoy the high art of sexual titillation.

The main hotel sits in the center of the Bondage Bay, just steps away from our clothing-optional beach. You will find everything you need in our unique hotel, including gourmet restaurants, unique shops, high-dollar gaming, and state-of-the-art dance clubs.

Many of Bondage Bay Hotel's suites include private play rooms. For an extra fee, we will create a personal space based on your needs and desires. We offer a delightful array of sexual aids, as well as your choice of BDSM furniture—from spanking benches to leather slings.

Our public dungeons are open 24/7 and are run by Doms and Dommes who are not only skilled in the arts of sexual torture, but are also trained Safety Agents. Our guests are our number one concern—you are always safe on our property.

We have many fun activities, but among our most popular events is the nightly slave auction hosted by the luscious Domme Lady Pink. All proceeds from the sales go to charitable causes. All the fun goes to you, either as the owner . . . or as the slave.

One
· · · · · ·

"**M**r. Devereaux, I'm not wearing *that*." Claire Williams handed her boss the rejected clothing and picked up her planner. She wasn't sure what bothered her more: that she wanted to wear the provocative clothing or that her gorgeous not quite former employer had asked her to put it on.

Pushing away such useless thoughts, Claire flipped open the planner to the current day, took out her ballpoint pen, and said, "You have an appointment with—"

"Claire." Did he *have* to say her name like that? Her boss had the sexiest voice—it was as silky smooth as a late-night DJ's.

Luscious Lucius, which was what other female employees called the annoying, arrogant, and handsome publisher of *Bad Boy Magazine*, crooked a finger at her. She obediently stepped into his personal space. He draped the tiny black leather skirt over her shoulder. "There is a dress code. You must wear appropriate attire."

She opened her mouth and he pressed a finger against her lips, his brown eyes sparkling with their usual mischief. Such an intimate gesture caused tingles in her belly. In fact, she had suffered the same kind of idiotic attraction to ol' Luscious as every other woman who came within three feet of him.

However, she had vehemently resisted being drawn in by his charm and good looks. Ha. Fat lot of good it had done to resist. Trying to stay out of Lucius's Lust Zone would be like the Earth trying to stop orbiting around the sun.

That was why she'd quit.

Until Lucius had drawn her back into a job that she'd vacated officially three days ago.

With a sigh, she plucked the skirt from her shoulder and tossed it onto the couch. It landed right next to a corset, which she had also rejected.

"You are my executive assistant," Lucius said, "which means you must assist me wherever I go."

Claire pressed her lips together so that she wouldn't point out that she had stopped being his executive assistant on Friday. But then he'd begged and bribed her to stay through this last *Bad Boy* project. So her services had been purchased for the weekend because he was footing the bill to a tropical paradise. He promised she would have more vacation than work.

He had failed to disclose the nature of the resort.

This kind of wild behavior was why she'd given her notice. She could no longer cope with the insanity of Lucius and *Bad Boy*. Well, that was the lie she told herself. Truthfully, she could no longer cope with her unprofessional emotions. She didn't want to be another name on Lucius's long list of heartbroken women.

She knew better than to be attracted to her boss. He appeared easygoing, but he had an iron will and iron control. Underneath his devil-may-care attitude hid a man who was dangerously sensual. Once, Claire had loved a man who'd promised her the same kind of wicked thrills.

But his idea of "wicked" and "thrill" had not matched hers. He hurt her—and destroyed what sexual confidence she had harbored.

She was very good at her job. But after two years of denying her feelings for Lucius and her needs as a woman, she'd had to let go. Her severance package was generous enough that she could take a couple months to reroute her career. She wanted to work somewhere less stressful—such as for the Pentagon or for Anna Wintour.

"Claire?" Lucius asked. "What are you thinking about?"

"About booking the next flight out of here." She sighed. "Call or text me. I'll handle any request from the hotel room."

Lucius lifted one eyebrow—his trademark look of amused incredulity. "They're closing one of the dungeons for two hours so we can do the photo shoot. It will be just you, me, the models, and the *Bad Boy* crew. You won't have to watch anyone get flogged . . . er, for real, okay?"

Oh crap. That was *exactly* what Claire didn't want to see. As it was, she had seen plenty already. In the hotel lobby, she saw a group of ladies who must've been in their sixties in purple panties and *nothing else* taking pictures under a sign that read PURPLE PANTY SOCIETY. Fleeing the sight, she'd hurried into the elevator only to find herself in a stranger situation. A tall man dressed in a custom-tailored Armani suit held chains in one fist. The chains led to the black studded collars of two women, who wore only black leather thongs and very high heels. They kneeled at his feet, heads bowed.

Unable to hold Lucius's gaze, Claire looked around at the opulent surroundings. The decor in Bondage Bay Resort seemed to be all about texture—leather ties on the velvet curtains, fluffy tassels on the silk pillows, dangling chains on the glass tables. The favored shade was black with splashes of primary colors.

Lucius and she had a luxurious two-bedroom suite on the top floor. Well, it had a third room, a private dungeon, which she had avoided. Heaven knew what was in *that* room. Otherwise, the suite was gorgeous and sumptuous. The balcony, accessed from the living room, overlooked the beach. While the sounds of the ocean were soothing, the view was anything but—actually, it was a lot of butts. The beach was "clothing optional."

Fantasyland

"Claire, wear the clothes. I agreed to the owner's terms when he allowed us to do the shoot." He looked her over and grinned. "Of course, you could always go naked."

"*Lucius.*" She swallowed the knot of pride clogging her throat. She always addressed him as Mr. Devereaux, not only because it was professional, but also because it annoyed the hell out of him. Everyone else called him Lucius without regard to his position or to his millions, which was exactly what he wanted. And Lucius Devereaux *always* got what he wanted. Feeling decidedly unnerved, she sank into the nearest chair and breathed deeply.

"Are you all right?" He grabbed the champagne bottle resting in a silver bucket on the coffee table. After he poured her a glass, he took the planner from her fierce grip and pressed the flute into her trembling hands. "You look ill. I hope that bastard Macintosh didn't give you his cold."

Macintosh was *Bad Boy's* number one photographer. He was the king of vices and loved his liquor, his women, and his cigars. He'd had a bout of sniffles this morning, but Claire knew Mac had done foliage shots and his plant allergies had kicked up. Despite his reaction to pollen, the man had never had a real sick day in his life.

Lucius crouched at her feet, one hand resting on her knee. He watched her, a smile playing about his full, sensual mouth. He was giving her an out—at least for a day or two. She could be a coward and play sick . . . or she could suck it up and do her damn job.

"I'll go to the dungeon," she said.

"That's my girl." Lucius's eyes flashed approval. His sexy smile knocked her on her ass. No wonder women fell at his feet and begged for his favors. *You are pathetic, Claire.* Lucius would never settle down. Why would he pick one woman to love forever when he could have as many women as he wanted and didn't have to love at all?

"You don't trust easily, do you?" he asked softly.

"It's much simpler than that, Mr. Devereaux. I don't trust at all."

"Why not?"

"What are you, my therapist?" she snapped. She drew in a shocked breath. Damn it. Why did the man keep pushing her? He seemed to delight in making her lose her temper. "Forgive me. I—I shouldn't have. . . . That was rude. I don't wish to discuss my life outside of our working relationship."

"That's a shame." Before she could respond, he stood up, his expression all business. "Shoot begins in an hour. I'll meet you there."

Claire downed a third glass of champagne. *I can do this.* She looked at herself in the full-length mirror. Her brown hair, glowing with her recent indulgence of highlights, curled around her shoulders. She wasn't one for lolling about in the sun, so she was pale, but her skin still had a healthy glow. She'd indulged in sparkly shadow to highlight her blue eyes and traded her usual coat of Chap-Stick for red lipstick.

Fantasyland

She put her hands on her hips and studied her reflection. The hip-hugging miniskirt and sexy calf boots were solid black; the black-and-teal striped corset paid serious homage to her 34C breasts. *I didn't realize I had that much cleavage.*

Well, at least now she looked like someone who belonged at the Bondage Bay Resort. If all of *Bad Boy's* employees were dressing the part, then she could do no less. Of course, she wondered how many of them were *playing* the part as well.

Claire arrived in the hotel lobby with twenty minutes to spare. When she spotted the little gift shop, she dropped in to grab a bottle of water and a tin of Altoids. Several shelves sported items travelers needed—toothbrushes and nail files, Pepto-Bismol and Imodium, potato chips and peanuts—as well as souvenirs.

On the way to the cash register to pay for her water and mints, she paused at a display of key chains: tiny floggers, handcuffs, red hearts, and—*Oh, lovely*—male genitalia. *C'mon! Who puts a teeny dick on their key chain?* Next to the display was a row of black coffee mugs. In fancy white typeface, one touted: I GOT TIED UP AT BONDAGE BAY RESORT.

She skipped over the shot glasses and snow globes. Unable to resist the sparkle of a rotating rack full of jeweled chokers, Claire plucked off a teal one. The color matched the teal stripes of her corset, and the three sparkling gems in the center complemented her diamond earrings.

"Hi there!" said the girl at the register. Her name tag read DAWN. "May I ask who the collar is for?"

Claire pulled out a credit card from her day planner. "It's mine."

"Wow. Your master let *you* pick it out?"

The girl sounded astonished. Damn. Claire didn't want to breech some jewelry-buying BDSM protocol. "He . . . er, picked it out and told me to . . . uh . . . buy it."

Dawn smiled. "My master picked out mine, too. I wore my blue collar for more than a year." She touched the silver-studded black leather strip around her throat. "When he presented me with this one, we had an official collaring ceremony at the resort—there's a chapel and a reception hall. Maybe one day you'll return for a ceremony, too."

Collaring ceremony? Claire wasn't sure how to respond, so she nodded and smiled as she signed the credit card receipt.

"Agreeing to a collar of consideration is a big step," Dawn chattered as she bagged the items. "There's no sweeter moment in life than when you offer yourself, body and soul, to the one who loves you."

"Yeah, that's a great moment, all right." Claire took the bag. "Thanks."

She hurried into the huge lobby, trying to remember Lucius's directions to the dungeon. Okay. There were the registration desk, the entrance to the restaurant, the entrance to the bar, the entrance to the beach, the hotel shop, the bank of elevators . . . which left her one option: the large hallway on the right. So down she went.

Ducking into a bathroom, she put on the choker. It looked really good. She freshened her lipstick and fluffed her hair. *Oh, vanity, thy name is Claire.* She stared at herself in the mirror, bemused. "What are you doing, you dolt? You don't want him to notice you. You want to get out of this job, remember?"

Sighing deeply, she left the bathroom. After wandering the hall for far too long, Claire started to panic. The hallway branched into several other hallways and there seemed to be a door every ten feet. Lucius had given her directions, but she couldn't make sense of her own notes. Sighing, she pulled out her cell phone. She loathed calling Lucius or Macintosh. She was not the *helpee*, she was the *helper*. She hated to be late, to be wrong, or to be lost.

Crap!

Two
· · · · · · ·

"**N**eed help, miss?"

Claire looked up, her finger hovering above Lucius's speed-dial number. A young man, probably in his early twenties, stood in front of her. He wore his blond hair in a crew cut. With his square jaw and buff body, he seemed almost militaristic. Except that he wore no shirt and his nipples were pierced with silver hoops, which were linked together by a thin silver chain. He also wore black leather pants and black biker boots with big silver buckles.

She gaped at his chest. "Doesn't that hurt?"

"Pain and pleasure are twins," he said.

"Right," she agreed, utterly unconvinced. He-Who-Shall-Not-Be-Named had tried to tell her the same load of shit. Once again, her gaze fell to the guy's chained pectorals.

"Do you want to pull on the chain?"

Yes, she did, but only to be perverse. She supposed that was the whole point of staying at a hotel called Bondage Bay.

"No, thanks." She smiled weakly. "Maybe next time."

"You bet." He looked her over, his gaze lingering on her choker. "Let me guess. Can't find the right room?"

"Yeah." Relief rushed through her. If he could tell her how to get to the dungeon, she'd make it in time and wouldn't have to call Lucius.

"Keep going until you reach the third hallway on the left. Go all the way to the end. The door is on the right. You better get going or you'll be late."

"Thanks." Claire hurried away, wondering how Nipple Boy knew she was going to be late. Oh, Lord, was he one of the models? Or one of *Bad Boy*'s many underlings?

When she reached the right door, she slipped inside, only to bounce face-first off the muscled chest of a mountainous man. He wore black leather pants and a black vest. *Doesn't anyone like blue around here?* He had long dark hair, dark eyes, and pierced lips. He grabbed her by the elbows as her planner, cell phone, and shopping bag went flying. "Whoa now, sugar," he drawled. "You just made it." He handed her a fan with a number on it. "Hurry on up to the stage now." He twirled her around and gently shoved her toward a row of platform steps.

"But my—"

"I got 'em, honey. I'll make sure you get 'em back after the auction."

Auction? Goddamn Lucius. Had he switched gears again? The man often changed times, days, locations, meetings—*anything* on a whim. Everyone hopped aboard the insanity train, too, because he made what should've been a pain in the ass into a party. She hated it when he got all impetuous. Internally grousing, she weaved through the models, looking for a familiar face. Where was Macintosh? For that matter, where was His Highness King Lucius?

"Stand here," demanded a woman dressed in a pink latex dress and thigh-high pink boots. Her entire body sparkled gold in the overhead lights. Even her long black hair glittered.

Claire blinked at her. "Oh. I'm not a—"

The woman snapped a pink whip at Claire's feet. *"Now."*

Meekly, Claire inserted herself into the spot between a tiny blonde in a nurse's costume and a redhead wearing nothing but a yellow miniskirt and black high heels.

"The auction will begin momentarily, ladies. You know the rules. Stand still. Hold your sign in your right hand, breast level. *Do not move* until you are purchased."

As Claire did what the woman said, foreboding sat heavy in her stomach. *This is so wrong.* Unless . . . Lucius had set her up. He liked teasing her, but he had never outright embarrassed her. Oh, God. Was he pranking her? With his twisted sense of humor, he might very well do some whacked-out bon voyage stunt.

When the curtains opened, would she see him, Macintosh, and other *Bad Boy* staff waiting for her to make a fool of herself? The more she thought about it, the more likely it seemed. Why else would he have insisted on her wearing this outfit? Suddenly, everything seemed rehearsed—from the young man finding her in the hall to the mountain man getting her on the stage.

I am going to kill you, Lucius.

Before she could decide whether to tough it out or to take the chicken's way out—right out of the line and off the stage—music blared and the curtains rolled back. As she looked out into the sea of people who packed the room, Claire felt the blood rush from her face. This wasn't the dungeon. And it wasn't an elaborate prank.

Claire's heart flipped over in her chest, then did the mambo up to her throat. Shit . . . oh *shit*.

A female voice purred, "Welcome, Doms and Dommes! Thank you for attending Lady Pink's nightly slave auction!"

"Claire's being auctioned off," said Mac, his English accent deliberately cockney, as he strolled into the dungeon ten minutes late. Mac was short, but buff, with a shaved head and pierced ears—three hoops in each lobe. He wore ripped jeans and a black T-shirt that read PORN STAR in big white letters.

Lucius's temper was about to snap. Mac thought arriving on time for anything was terribly droll, but Claire would get hit by a car and still drag her carcass into the office rather than be a millisecond late. But she *was* late and he was damned worried.

Had she booked that flight after all?

"Damn it, Mac! I know you're the best photographer in the biz, but we only have two hours and you're costing—" Lucius stared at his friend's smug expression. "What did you say?"

"Your executive assistant is on Lady Pink's auction block. She looks delish, I must say." Mac whistled. "It's across the hallway. I peeked in to see what's what."

For a moment, Lucius simply could not wrap his mind around the idea that Claire had volunteered for a BDSM slave auction. "What the bloody hell is she doing?"

"Sellin' herself to the highest bidder." Mac grinned. "What's wrong, mate? Afraid someone else will get your submissive?"

"Shut up."

Mac laughed, unafraid of Lucius's ire. "Here you are, a Dom without a sub. And there she is—"

"A woman who doesn't recognize her own nature." Lucius rubbed his temples. "She's not mine. Hell, she wants to get away from me so badly she quit her job!"

Mac slapped Lucius on the shoulder. "I was only havin' you on, Lucius. I bet our Claire got her directions mixed up. Maybe she thought we'd changed the shoot's location." Mac shrugged. "Not out of the realm of possibility, mate. You're as likely to change your mind as the sun is to shine."

That explanation made a helluva lot more sense. Claire

had not shown an interest in the BDSM lifestyle. But even if she'd decided it was time to unleash her inner naughty girl, she wouldn't have ditched work.

Lucius strode toward the door, but Mac grabbed him by the arm. "Hold on there. Don't embarrass yourself or Claire by doing something impetuous." Mac gestured to the rack of costumes they'd brought in for the models. "If you want to rescue your damsel, you gotta look the part of the knight."

"Are you suggesting that I buy Claire?"

"It's what you've been trying to do since she quit."

"That's crossing the line," said Lucius through clenched teeth. He hated that his friend was right. He'd been trying to figure out a way to keep Claire near him. She was sensitive to his moods, remembered what he liked and what he didn't, and often gave him the kind of hard-ons that required cold showers. He sensed her natural submissive tendencies, but had never pushed the issue with her.

Until now.

When she'd given him two weeks' notice, he'd been shell-shocked. Maybe that was why he'd done everything in his power to get her to Bondage Bay. He'd been telling himself that he only wanted to convince her to stay as his assistant.

But maybe he'd really been hoping for this kind of opportunity. He had a chance to explore a deeper relationship with her. *No.* This was crazy. He would simply buy her anonymously and let her go. Unless she wanted to be his slave . . . Yeah, if she accepted him as her Dom, then he would take her.

She'll never agree. Why would Claire show her vulnerability and pain to a stranger when she wouldn't open up to him? Surely she knew that he cared deeply for her.

"Better get going, mate," Mac said.

Lucius glanced at the row of black leather outfits. "Fine. I'll do whatever it takes to save her, but you stay here and take some damn pictures."

"Aye, aye, Cap'n."

Claire had tried twice to leave, but Lady Pink snapped the whip on her exposed upper thigh. It stung like hell. She desperately wanted to tell someone that a huge mistake had been made. Lady Pink was busy listing the attributes of the slaves. Honestly, Claire really didn't want any more of the woman's attention.

Bad Boy had agreed not to interrupt ongoing activities. As much as Claire wanted to leap off the stage and run away, she didn't want to do something that would affect *Bad Boy* or Lucius negatively. Besides, she was a little scared of Lady Pink. And she was a lot scared of being someone's sexual property.

So she decided that she would negotiate with whoever bought her. The "sales" were really charitable donations, and she was a sucker for supporting good causes. All she had to do was explain to her purchaser that she was not a slave and offer to reimburse the price paid. She'd figure out something to tell Lucius about her late arrival. Then she could forget about this humiliating experience.

"Sold!" purred Lady Pink. "Our first sale of the evening, ladies and gentlemen, for two thousand three hundred dollars." She drew the pink whip over the young woman's shoulder. "Step forward, slave."

The woman moved out of the lineup. She was dressed in a red miniskirt and thigh-high boots. Her small breasts were barely covered by a strip of red fabric. She wore a hair band that sported two red horns.

"What's your name?" asked Lady Pink.

"Devil Girl."

Lady Pink gestured to someone on the side of the stage. A man strode toward them. He wore an elaborate yellow mask that looked like a sunburst; his vinyl outfit had gradient shades of yellow, orange, and red.

"This is your master, Devil Girl. He has purchased you for the next twenty-four hours. Do you agree to be his?"

"Yes."

"Show your master homage."

Devil Girl kneeled before the tall sun god and kissed his booted feet.

"Does she meet your approval, master?" asked Lady Pink.

"Yes," said the man.

"Everyone knows the rules." Lady Pink smiled seductively and snapped the whip in the air. "A master and his slave must entertain us. Whet our appetites, beloved ones. Give us a *hot* scene."

The crowd cheered and clapped.

Claire felt her stomach drop to her toes. What fresh hell was this?

"Stand up," demanded the master.

His slave stood immediately and kept her eyes cast down.

"Turn around so that your back faces the audience."

Again, Devil Girl did exactly as the man directed.

"Bend over and grab your ankles."

The woman bent over and wrapped her hands around the red boots.

Claire watched in breathless anticipation. What would the master demand next? And why was the woman complying so readily? She didn't seem to mind being bossed around at all. Claire didn't want to contemplate the idea that her own reaction was skewed. Her heart pounded and sweat dotted her brow.

The master flipped up Devil Girl's skirt and revealed her naked ass to the people watching. Claire's face went hot with embarrassment as she realized the woman wore no underwear at all.

"Would you like an instrument of torture?" asked Lady Pink. She wheeled over a tray filled with items that looked like surgical tools. Claire also noticed a couple floggers, a selection of dildos, several thin metal rods, and a Taser.

Her gaze switched to the poor woman. Claire wondered how Devil Girl could tolerate standing in that position. All the blood was rushing to her head, and surely, she would pass out.

The master chose a slim metal piece that was flat and about as long as his arm. He held it at one end, then placed it across Devil Girl's exposed buttocks.

A hush descended on the crowd. Seconds ticked by and Claire realized the man was making his slave wait. Was Devil Girl dreading the impact? Or would she relish it?

Whack! The metal slapped Devil Girl's pale flesh and left a thin red welt. Claire nearly swallowed her tongue.

Whack! Whack! Whack!

The girl didn't flinch, but Claire did. Then she swore she heard a low moan. *She's enjoying it!* Claire's heart thundered in her chest. She was willing to go through the charade to a point, but the idea of doing BDSM play with a complete stranger terrified her.

It also excited her.

Whoa. What? No. Okay. Yes. But it only intrigued her a *little.* Had her ex-lover been right about her? Did she deny her sexual needs because they seemed wrong? No. Phillip pushed and pushed until she'd caved and then . . . Well, it had ended badly. If Phillip had truly loved her, he wouldn't have prodded her into those circumstances.

The master whacked the woman's ass another five times. Claire tried to control her breathing. God, it was hot in here.

She didn't dare move, not with Lady Pink so close and her whip so ready.

Finally the master finished. He traced every welt lovingly, then flipped down the skirt. "You may stand."

Devil Girl rose, standing still, and waited. The master rubbed her ass and said, "You have pleased me."

Claire saw the flash of pleasure in Devil Girl's eyes as she smiled. The master took her by the hand and led her off the stage.

The crowd applauded loudly while some whistled and others shouted. When the merriment settled down, Lady Pink sauntered behind Claire and wrapped an arm around her waist. "Take a look at this trim and beautiful goddess! Is she not all that you desire?"

Lady Pink brushed her hand over the teal choker. "Her master must adore her! He has blessed her with a collar of consideration and yet he allows her to play with a special bidder."

She pushed Claire forward and shouted, "Come on, Doms and Dommes. Who will bid on our next lovely slave?"

Three
· · · · · · · · ·

"Five hundred dollars!"

"One thousand!"

"Fifteen hundred!"

"They want you," purred Lady Pink. She stepped past Claire and snapped the whip. "Fifteen hundred? Is that all you will pay for this goddess to be yours?"

"Fifteen thousand."

Claire almost swallowed her tongue. Due to the bright stage lights, she couldn't really see individual faces. The deep voice of the male bidder seemed to be farther back in the room.

"Sixteen thousand," said another male voice, this one had a gruff English accent.

"Twenty thousand," came the counteroffer.

"Twenty-one thousand."

"Fifty thousand!" roared the first man.

"Going once, going twice . . . sold!" yelled Lady Pink. "Come to the stage, master, and claim what is yours!" She smiled broadly at Claire. "I've never sold a slave for that much. He must really want you."

While they waited for the buyer to make his way through the throngs of people, Lady Pink titillated the crowd with details about the next girl up for auction.

Fifty thousand dollars! Claire tried not to panic. Oh, crap! No way could she pay off a fifty-thousand-dollar charitable donation. She might have to commit herself to being the slave of her mystery man.

Now why did that option cause delicious shivers? She wasn't into BDSM and she hated mind games. Thanks to Phillip she'd been mind fucked enough, thank you. She didn't need some jerk telling her what to do and where to go and—

"Welcome, master," said Lady Pink.

Nervously, Claire looked at the tall man dressed head to toe in black leather, including a black hood with only holes for his eyes and mouth. Her heart pounded furiously. The way his clothes fit indicated a well-muscled body. She wondered what he looked like under his mask.

"Slave! Step forward and show homage to your owner."

Claire hesitated a second too long. The pink whip whistled ominously toward her thigh, but the man grabbed the Domme's wrist.

"Nobody punishes my slave." His voice was low and

slightly rough. It reminded her of Christian Bale's voice when he donned the mask of Batman.

Lady Pink's mouth thinned and her eyes flashed with challenge. "She has not acquiesced to be yours."

"You haven't given her the opportunity."

He dropped the woman's wrist. Then he looked at Claire. "What is your name?"

Oh, hell. She couldn't give him her real name. Thinking of her favorite Disney movie, she said, "My name is Belle."

"Vous êtes belle, ma fleur."

You are beautiful, my flower. His French was flawless. She dropped her head in acknowledgment and said, *"Merci."*

"Do you accept me as your master?"

The question hung in the air, glistening with promise. Doubt nibbled at her, but she could only offer one answer. "Yes."

"Entertain us!" crowed Lady Pink, snapping her whip in the air.

"We will not do a scene," announced Claire's new master. "Come with me, Belle."

He turned around, fully expecting Claire to adhere to his command. What could she do but follow? As she did so, she noticed that the man who'd purchased her had a really nice ass. Gak! What was wrong with her? Well, hell, just because Lucius was permanently off her menu didn't mean she couldn't consider the other entrées.

When they got off the stage, a woman handed Claire her day planner, cell phone, and shopping bag.

Hurrying to catch up with her master, she touched his arm. She could tell by his sudden stillness that she had violated some kind of slave-master etiquette. He turned to her and she felt the weight of his pointed stare.

"There's been a mistake," she said. "I'm not a slave. I ended up on the stage by accident."

"What if I told you, Belle, that there were no accidents?"

She stopped short of rolling her eyes. "I'd say you were full of shit."

"Interesting answer." He studied her for a moment.

With his face covered, she couldn't see his expression and his eyes offered no clue about his thoughts.

Finally, he said, "You wish to break our agreement?"

"I can pay you back the fifty thousand dollars—"

He shook his head. "I'm not talking about the money. I'm talking about your acceptance of me as your master for the next twenty-four hours."

Claire's eyes widened. "I . . . that is . . ." Her heart turned over in her chest. She clenched her hands to stop them from shaking. "I don't know how to be . . ."

The rest of the words died in her throat.

"A submissive."

She nodded.

"You don't have a master. Why are you wearing a blue collar?"

"I bought it in the gift shop because it matched my corset." Her cheeks flamed as she confessed her vanity. "I was supposed to go to a photo shoot. In fact, I'm really late. My boss is going to give me the third degree."

"Perhaps I will."

Claire peered up at him. "What?"

The mouth hole wasn't large enough to show his lips, but she realized he was smiling. "I'm teasing you." He chuckled. "You would be so delicious, Belle. But I do not take the unwilling."

"The money . . ."

"I don't care about the money," he said with a shrug. "But I am disappointed about losing you." He cupped her face and brushed her cheek with his thumb. "It's a shame you don't wish to explore your true nature."

"Someone already tried what you're offering to do," she admitted. "Believe me, it's not my true nature."

"I'm sorry." His hand dropped away and Claire felt suddenly bereft. "He was not the one for you."

"But you are?"

"We will never know."

Her stomach squeezed. He sounded so disappointed. She opened her planner and unhooked the pen. "I feel just awful about this whole thing. Here, give me your cell phone number so I can call you to discuss repayment. Fifty grand is a lot of money. It might take me a while to procure funds."

"You will not repay me the money."

Mortified by his stern tone, she stuck the pen into its

holder. Her face heated with embarrassment as she looked at the floor. "Okay."

"If you were mine," he said, "I would punish you for disobeying me."

Claire's mouth dropped open. *Punish* her? She thought of Devil Girl's spanking and couldn't decide if the idea was ridiculous or a very dark turn-on.

Claire's master stepped into her personal space, his boots toe-to-toe with hers. He tilted her chin, forcing her gaze upward. Her breath hitched at his intensity.

"Oh, yes, *ma fleur.* I would punish you for not listening. I would bend you over my knee and I would spank your sweet, firm ass. And you would take every hit quietly and obediently." He leaned very close and whispered, "Wouldn't you?"

For a moment, she felt the helplessness inspired by Phillip's attempts to control her. He had never called what he did BDSM, but a whip by any other name was still a whip.

She couldn't face the idea that she might enjoy what this man offered—that he wanted to give her something different, an experience meant for her pleasure. *I don't care what he says about my damned nature. I won't let anyone hurt me again.*

"I asked you a question, Belle."

"Stop," she said, her voice warbling. "Please."

"As you wish." Just like that, the spell he had woven with his words and his presence was broken. He stepped back. "A master always listens to his submissive."

"You mean you would just stop because I say so?" Claire swallowed the knot clogging her throat.

"Of course. If your former lover mistreated you, it was not because you deserved it." He looked at her, and once again she got the impression he was smiling. "Belle, I would worship you. I would show you how to conquer your fears, how to open yourself to the wonder and beauty of your own soul."

"By spanking me?"

He laughed. "That's only part of it. But you are not mine, are you? If you change your mind, meet me tonight in the lobby bar at nine p.m. I'll be on the right side, third booth."

"And if I don't show up?"

"You will be the one who got away." He raised his hands in a placating gesture. "No harm, no foul."

"What should I wear?" The question popped out before Claire could fully form the thought.

He seemed pleased that she'd asked.

"You will wear a red dress and red high heels. You will not put on a bra, panties, or hose. Wear light makeup with red lipstick. Leave your hair down. No jewelry. Bring your ID but no purse. You will not need money."

"How can I trust you?"

"There is only one way for you to find out." He took her hand and pressed his lips against it. "Au revoir, Belle." He turned and walked away.

Claire stared after him, absently massaging where he'd

kissed her hand. One question echoed in her mind: Did she have the nerve to show up for their rendezvous?

"You threw up?"

Claire flinched at the suspicion in Lucius's words. *Liar, liar, pants on fire.* She had waited until she got back to her hotel room before she called her boss. Pride goeth before the fall, all right. She couldn't admit to Lucius that she'd been late because some guy had bought her as a sex slave. Since Lucius had given her an out earlier in the day, she grabbed the illness excuse and gave it to him, even though it made her feel guilty and heartsick.

"I'm really not feeling well. I'm sorry I didn't call sooner."

"That's okay. I prefer not to hear the sounds of vomiting," said Lucius. "How about dinner tonight? I'll bring you soup and crackers. We have to do a few night shots while the weather is clear. I could come up about nineish."

"Uh . . . well . . . y'know, I'll probably turn in early." Claire clutched the phone and closed her eyes. Oh, God, she was so going to hell. She had never, ever told a fib to Lucius.

Somewhere between leaving Lady Pink's auction and arriving at her hotel room, she had decided to meet her master. She could hardly believe it, but here she was, already thinking of him as her *master*.

The very idea of being dominated sent both panic and desire winding through her. Maybe he was what she needed to make a clean break from her feelings for Lucius. Was it wrong to want to be free of the man who could never love her? Was it more wrong to crave the pleasure promised by the man in the black mask?

"Order room service," said Lucius. "I'll check on you later."

"No," she practically yelled. Sheesh. *Calm down, Claire.* "I mean, that's okay. I'm taking Nyquil. It'll knock me out for the night. I bet I'll feel right as rain tomorrow."

"I hope so," he said. "I only have you for two more days. I will miss you, Claire."

"Your new assistant will be everything you need."

"No, she won't," he said softly, "because she won't be you."

Four
·········

L ucius flipped the cell phone shut and tossed it to Mac.
He took off the black leather mask and combed his fingers through his hair. In the dungeon, everyone was packing
up gear, clothing, and props. The models had already left.

He had just finished telling Mac what had transpired at
the auction when Claire called and lied her ass off about
not feeling well. He smiled. She had never taken a sick day
in the two years she'd worked for him. And she had never
lied.

She must really want to be with her mystery man. Lucius
frowned. It rankled him that she would consider sex games
with a complete stranger, but hadn't shown an iota of sexual
interest in him. In fact, she went out of her way to behave as
if she didn't find him at all attractive.

"You're a cruel one," said Mac without rancor, "teasin' our Claire that way."

"I needed to find out if she was going to show up tonight. Y'know, I think I'm jealous of myself. Or rather, I'm jealous of the man Claire thinks I am."

"Just tell her you want her more'n you wanted anyone ever, and drop this whole charade." Mac shook his head. "You're playin' a dangerous game, mate."

"I know that," said Lucius irritably. After buying Claire, he had planned to walk away. He'd been positive she had no interest in being a slave to anyone. An excellent assistant, she accomplished every task given to her, but she wasn't one to shut her mouth if she thought he was fucking up.

To his shock, she had been genuinely intrigued by a D/s relationship. And he sure as hell hadn't counted on finding out that some asshole had already tried to dominate her—and had managed to hurt her deeply.

"If I told Claire how I feel, she would think that I just wanted to fuck her," said Lucius. "She would not only say no—she would kick me in the balls and hit me in the face with her day planner."

"That planner of hers would knock your teeth out," said Mac. "Still, you might be better off goin' the honest route. If she finds out you're her new master, there won't be enough pieces left of you for a proper funeral."

"Not enough for an open casket," agreed Lucius. He looked at the hood he'd worn. It was hot and uncomfortable, but he had one in his room that he could use tonight.

Tonight. His dick was already hardening at the mere idea of Claire submitting to him. He could peel aside all those prickly layers and find her vulnerabilities. Given enough time, he could awaken her to new pleasures and help her conquer her fears. A night with Claire wouldn't be enough—but it was all he had.

Mac was right. Lucius was playing a dangerous game with Claire. But if things turned out right, they'd both get what they wanted.

He was assuming that Claire actually wanted him. They could be so much more to each other if she would only reach out to him. *Why don't you trust me, Claire? Why don't you trust anyone?*

He meant to find out. Now that the game was started, he would finish it. Even if Claire wanted out afterward, at least he would give her one gift. When he was done, she would know exactly what she wanted and how to get it.

In submitting to him, she would banish her demons and find pleasure in serving her master.

The hotel bar was called Enchained. Claire had gone to three different stores to find the red dress and high heels. Luckily, the hotel had no shortage of clothing stores.

In her job, she wore muted colors: tans and creams, browns and blacks. She owned several "little black dresses," but not a single item in her wardrobe was red.

As requested, she wore nothing under her dress. Her legs were smooth and tan, thanks to an earlier spa treatment. Her hair was worn straight, without adornment, and she'd brushed it until it shone. She carried her driver's license, and she wore very, very red lipstick.

At eight fifty-nine, she walked into the bar. It was crowded, filled with men and woman in various states of dress and undress. Most wore black leather and some carried riding crops and whips.

She turned right, pushed her way through the people, and presented herself at the third booth.

Her master sat on the left side, drinking a flute of champagne. He wore a black cloth mask that covered his head and most of his face. His shirt was red and his dress pants black. He looked very handsome, even though she could only see the tip of his nose, his full lips, and his square jaw.

He put down his glass, looked at his watch, then up at her. "You're right on time, Belle." He studied her leisurely. "You look exquisite—like a beautiful present. I look forward to unwrapping you."

Claire found it incredibly arousing that she had pleased him. Fear and longing entwined in a dance that made her stomach flutter. She feared what he might demand of her, but she also longed for the kind of pleasure he could bestow on her. She only prayed that she'd made the right choice. Phillip told her once that he'd sensed her submissive nature. He had promised to break down her barriers, but all he really did was break *her*.

"Sit down."

Until her master uttered the words, Claire hadn't realized that she'd been instinctively waiting for his directive. She looked at him, uncertain.

"Belle." His tone was sharp.

"I don't mean to disobey," she said softly, "but where should I sit?"

His lips curved into a gentle smile. "I'm sorry, Belle. I was not specific, was I? You require clarity." He scooted out of the booth and gestured for her to join him.

She slid across the vinyl seat until her hip grazed the wall. She toyed with her driver's license as he sat next to her.

"Give me your ID."

She handed it over and he tucked it into his front pants pocket. He sipped his champagne, offering her none as he looked around the bar. Claire was unsure if she was allowed to talk or to move.

"Sit close to me," he said. "Flip your dress up."

Claire's heart pounded furiously as she moved nearer to him. Her hands shook violently as they gripped the edge of her dress. *This is crazy. I can't just . . . oh, God. What am I doing?*

"Are you thinking that you made a mistake?"

Claire looked up into the knowing gaze of her master. She nodded.

"You can leave right now," he said. "Or you can lift your dress and show me your pussy."

His words shocked her. But her body reacted in a far

different manner. Her nipples hardened and she got instantly wet. She hated to admit it, but she was enjoying his domination.

Sucking in a deep breath, she pulled up the material and revealed her Brazilian-waxed cunt. He glanced down, then nodded. She started to re-cover herself, but he said, "No. Leave it."

Even though she felt extremely vulnerable with her dress shoved up to her hips, she was determined to see this experience through. The table was so big and the lighting so dim, it was doubtful that anyone walking by could see her bared thighs.

"Put your hands flat on the table."

Claire put her palms against the burnished wood.

Minutes ticked by. He said nothing to her. He sipped the champagne and watched the people around them, some involved in their own games. And while he observed others, she observed him. The bar was dimly lit, but she could still see his handsome profile. She hoped that before their game was over, he would reveal his identity.

Finally, he turned to her. "You're doing very well."

"Thank you."

"'Thank you, master,'" he corrected. "When you speak to me, you must call me 'master.' Understand?"

"Yes, master."

"What a good girl you are, Belle."

Pleasure curled through her. Claire found it almost unbelievable that his praise meant so much to her. Yes, there was satisfaction in doing well, but there was also sexual titillation. Her body thrummed with growing need. Her nipples poked against the soft material of her dress and her pussy clenched.

And he hadn't even touched her.

"Would you like some champagne, Belle?"

Claire nodded. He lifted the flute to her lips and she sipped the bubbly, sweet liquid. "Thank you, master."

"You're welcome."

He finished off the drink. Then he said, "Spread your legs."

Her pulse stuttered, but she did as he commanded. She nearly swallowed her tongue when he reached between her thighs and stroked one finger up one side of her labia and down the other.

"You're wet," he said. His voice went low and hot. "I bet you taste good."

Why don't you find out? But she didn't dare utter those words. In this world, she belonged to him. She was not the aggressor. She needed only to relax and he would care for her.

His finger delved between her folds, teasing the sensitive flesh. Her palms tingled as she kept them pressed against the table; her hands started to sweat. Even so, she didn't move them lest her disobedience cause her master to stop touching her.

She wanted to squirm and to moan and to beg, but she

said nothing and kept her ass planted against the vinyl. He didn't look at her, but she knew she had his attention. God knew that he had hers.

Moisture beaded her forehead and she bit her lower lip as a moan threatened to escape from her throat.

"You will not come," he said as his finger diddled her clit. "Not until I tell you."

She wanted to protest the very idea of being brought to orgasm in the middle of a crowded bar, but she couldn't get words to form.

Excitement built in her pussy as he stroked her faster and faster. She sucked in a breath and her eyes fluttered closed.

"Open your eyes," he said. "Look at me."

She turned dazed eyes to him.

"You are so beautiful," he said. "I can't wait to see you come."

Her breath quickened and her heart pounded furiously. Pleasure coiled tighter and tighter. She could let go at any second.

"Put your arms around me."

Claire gladly lifted her palms off the table and wrapped her arms around her master. Doing so shifted her position slightly, but it didn't affect her master's expert pleasuring of her clit.

He moved closer, as if accepting her hug. She was startled when he leaned down and lightly bit her left nipple through her dress. Whoa! Pleasure-pain zapped straight to her cunt.

He nuzzled his way up her neck. "Look at me."

She drew back far enough so she could lock eyes with him. Her entire body thrummed with need. Oh, God. She teetered on the edge. She wanted to beg for release, but even more, she wanted his permission.

Oh, hell. It was true. She craved his dominion. She wanted to submit to him. It felt right. And oh so good.

"Belle," he whispered, keeping his gaze on hers, "I want you to come."

He leaned down and bit her nipple again. The intensity of that action pushed her over.

Endless waves of bliss crashed through her. Her arms tightened around his shoulders as she swallowed her cries of completion. Her whole body shuddered as he cupped her mound; her pussy convulsed and wept against his hand.

He gave her a few moments to recover, but he had made her shatter in more ways than one. She felt swallowed up by the emotions rioting through her still trembling form. She felt so vulnerable right now, and more than a little worried about her ease with this stranger.

"Come here," he said as he pulled her onto his lap. He kissed her—a sweet, brief press against her lips. "How do you feel?"

"Incredible." Orgasmic tremors still rocked her pussy. "Thank you, master."

He smiled. "*Ma fleur*, we have only begun our journey

together." He pushed her hair behind her ears. "Are you ready for the next part?"

"Yes, master."

With her still clutched in his grasp, he scooted off the bench. As he stood up, he scooped her into his arms and carried her out of the bar.

Five

· · · · · · · ·

Her master carried her through the lobby. Claire felt her cheeks heat with embarrassment as they gained the attention of guests and staff. *They've probably seen everything.* She looked at him, feeling unaccountably shy.

He was smiling. "You look so lovely when you blush."

"I've never been literally swept off my feet."

"It is my honor to carry you."

His courtly words charmed her and she returned his smile.

He walked past the bank of elevators, which took guests to the upper floors. As he headed toward the main hallway, her eyes widened. For a panicked moment, she thought he might take her to a public dungeon. Not only was she not ready to show others these new truths she was discovering about herself—she was afraid she might run into someone from *Bad Boy*.

Instead, he rounded a corner and walked down a short hallway. Within minutes they arrived at a single elevator. A guard stood on duty, his brawny arms crossed as he watched their approach.

No words were exchanged. The guard nodded to her master and pushed the button. The shining gold doors parted and her master carried her inside.

Dipping her toward the panel, he said, "Push the red button."

"I hope nothing explodes," she murmured as she punched the unnumbered circle.

He laughed as he righted her, bestowing a kiss on her collarbone. Then, slowly, he lowered her to the floor. Their clothes were thin barriers, hiding neither her turgid nipples nor his hard-on. She realized that before the night was over, he would strip off more than her clothes.

He would strip her defenses.

Claire felt the sculpted muscles and delicious heat of his chest as she pressed against him. Her heels scraped against the marble; the only other sound was their intermingled breath.

"See the railing?" he asked.

Claire looked at the gold rail. It separated the polished wood lining the lower half of the car from the upper mirrors.

"Yes, master."

"Go to the railing, hold on to it, and then lean down and bare your ass."

Her heart revved as she moved away from him, from his warmth and his safety. She wondered how far he would try to push her in this game of theirs. And she wondered how far she could go. She had disappointed Phillip so badly. *You're not cut out for this, Claire. You're too vanilla.*

Then why was she so turned on? Why was she staying here, instead of running away?

I need this.

Claire stopped a half foot from the bar and leaned over, dragging her dress over her ass. Then she wrapped clammy fingers around the cold metal and waited.

In the mirror she saw the fear and need in her own gaze. She saw him, too. His mask couldn't hide his hunger for her. The air seemed to thicken with tension, with heat, with expectation. Her heart stuttered as desire built low and heavy in her belly. He leaned over and pressed another glowing button on the panel.

The elevator slowed to a stop.

Her stomach dove to her toes as she realized that she was trapped with him in a twelve-by-twelve box. A ready-made cage. She couldn't escape from him in here—or from her own desires.

His eyes flickered to hers in the mirror. "Look at the floor."

She did as he demanded, though she preferred to watch

him. She wanted to know what he planned. The thought of not knowing what he would do next was both thrilling and frustrating.

"I told you that a master always listens to his submissive. We play these games for pleasure, but also to address certain emotional needs. Needs that can only be met when we give each other absolute trust."

She felt him move behind her. Licking her lips nervously, she sucked in an unsteady breath. She hadn't realized that a connection between two people could be like this—beyond mere sex, beyond even mere relationship. Phillip's abuse had been disguised; he hadn't cared about her pleasure. Already this man had proven he was different.

And Lucius? For an aching moment, she wished he was behind her. She wished *he* would dominate her. That he would love her. But that would never happen. She wanted more than he could give. Better never to know his kiss or his touch than to have it for a short while and spend her days yearning for more.

"Sometimes, the situations get intense," continued her master. "An experienced Dom will push you past that point where you believe your boundaries lie. You may think you cannot meet another demand, another punishment, another sensual torture, but I assure you, Belle, that you can."

Claire's breathing was uneven and her arms tingled from their stretched position. Whatever she'd gotten herself into with this man, she wanted it. But to hand over her trust along with her body for one night of playing together—that, she wasn't sure she could do.

"If you feel that anything I do to you is approaching your breaking point, say 'yellow.' Do you understand?"

"Yes, master."

"If anything I ask is beyond your endurance, say 'red.' Do you understand?"

"Yes, master."

"You are in my domain. I own you. You will do what I say when I say it or I will punish you." One finger dragged down her buttock. "You are mine to do with as I wish and you will remain mine until dawn. Do you understand?"

"Yes, master."

Oh, God. Was he going to play with her all night? She had to be at a breakfast meeting at eight a.m. But she didn't want sleep as much as she wanted to be here with him.

"Good." He pulled down her dress. "Stand up."

She let go of the railing and straightened. Her arms and legs prickled uncomfortably. She looked into the mirror and found her master staring at her.

"Did I tell you to stop looking at the floor?"

Her heart turned over in her chest. Her belly clenched with dread as she returned her gaze to the floor. "I'm sorry."

"That's two infractions."

Shit. What had she done to get a second demerit? Her thoughts raced, and then it came to her: She hadn't called him "master." Claire realized he'd been gentle with her so far. His explanation of safe words had been a warning that things between them were going to get intense. She hated that she had disappointed him. Fear curled in her stomach. What would he do to her?

"You must be punished," he said softly. "Bend over and hold your ankles."

Heart pounding, Claire did exactly as he said. Once again, he flipped up her dress. What was he—

He smacked her ass hard with his open palm.

Ouch! She swallowed her cry of outrage.

He smacked her again. Fuck! That hurt! Yet her pussy clenched and moisture seeped from the folds. He landed a third blow. The sting vibrated to her very core. *Oh, God.* She kept her gaze on the floor and pressed her lips together.

He spanked her twice more, leaving her ass raw. Tears fell on the floor between her heels. Her throat knotted as she tried to drag in shuddering breaths. Her body couldn't decide between pleasure and pain, so it went with both. The sensations confused her.

"Stand up."

She straightened. Her legs hurt and her ass throbbed, but she kept her arms at her sides and her gaze on the floor.

"Turn around and look at me."

She didn't want to, but she didn't want another spanking, either. Slowly, she faced him and dragged her gaze to his face. His eyes didn't reveal any emotion and the damn mask hid his expression.

Fantasyland

"Close your eyes."

For a moment, she considered screaming "red" and ending this crazy night. Screw him and his head trips. Then her stubborn nature reasserted itself. He wouldn't break her, damn it.

She closed her eyes. It was, she realized, a sign of trust. She was giving him permission to do as he liked. Not because he wanted it, but because she wanted it. For the first time, she understood that control rested in her hands as the submissive.

He cupped her face and brushed his lips across hers. "You took your punishment well. I'm proud of you."

The dread and disappointment winding through her like poisonous snakes dissipated in an instant. She had pleased him!

He held her hand; then he pushed the button that released the elevator. In moments, the doors opened and he led her into a marble foyer.

Obviously, they were in one of the ultraluxurious penthouse suites. If paying fifty thousand dollars for a one-day slave wasn't enough of a hint about his finances, then the size and luxury of the suite stated it loudly.

Only one lamp glowed in the living room. The rest of the suite was dark. Even the curtains were closed. He led her past the big, blocky furniture and toward a spiral staircase.

"Hold on to the rail," he said as he let go of her hand. "In those heels, you could trip on the stairs."

He started up first and she followed him. At the top was a single door, which he opened. The room beyond was pitch-black. Generally, Claire wasn't afraid of the dark or of confined spaces, but she was still nervous about entering that utter blackness.

She licked her lips. "Is that your bedroom?"

"It's my dungeon."

Her fingers, which were still curled around the top of the railing, gripped the cool metal. "I've only been in one," she said. "But I didn't stay very long."

Phillip had taken her to a public dungeon once, and the experience had scared the hell out of her. That had also been the end of their relationship. If she was so vanilla, why did her fantasies always put her on her knees at the feet of a strong male? Her heart pounded. *What do I really want?*

"Are you scared?" her master asked.

She nodded.

"Are you willing to face your fears?"

That was the million-dollar question. Letting go of the rail, she sucked in a steadying breath.

Then she walked into the room.

After a few steps, her knees smacked into something low and wooden. She stopped, leaning down to rub her protesting kneecaps. Her master entered the room. She heard the slide of a drawer, the scrape of a matchstick, and then light flickered in the darkness.

He lit several candles on a side table. Their low flames

didn't penetrate very far into the large room, but she could see several pieces of strange furniture. On the wall nearest the candle was a series of floggers and riding crops.

Her master walked to her and cupped her face. "You are brave and strong and spirited."

"Thank you, master." Her gaze flicked down to the item that had so painfully stalled her progress.

"It's a spanking table," he explained. "See how this part is lower than the large surface? That's where you kneel as you lay down. Your waist is supported by this narrow piece of straight wood and your torso drapes across the angled tabletop."

Claire considered the table. For a moment, she imagined herself splayed against it in the way he described. Her bare skin would press against the black leather. Her ass would be angled just right for penetration, too. Her heart stuttered as she considered that scenario. And would he spank her? Would he use the flat of his hand or choose one of those floggers? Her stomach squeezed.

"You're interested in the table," he said softly. "I think you want to lay on it, *ma fleur*. Yes, it would be a treat to strap your ankles and your wrists to the table. You would look so beautiful shackled to it, so helpless to my every whim."

Desire fluttered through her. Yes, she wanted to experience the pleasure to be had on the spanking table. She would take the whipping, damn it. She wanted to be worthy of him, to show her master that she could take his punishment and earn her pleasure.

"Do you want the table, Belle?"

Claire's legs wiggled like Jell-O. Her body quivered at the sensual promise in his words. She would conquer the doubts and worries still plaguing her. As of now, she was leaving behind the idea that she would walk away from this man. She was his. At least for tonight.

Claire dropped to her knees, lowering her head as she gazed at the tips of his shoes. Her heart pounded furiously as she said, "Yes, master. Please."

Six
· · · · · · · ·

When Claire sank to the floor and offered her obedience, Lucius admitted to himself the truth: He was in love with her.

He'd lusted after Claire since the day he'd hired her. He'd flirted with her outrageously, but she ignored him. Any time he tested the waters, she rolled her eyes and pretended not to notice his attempts to impress her.

God! Just one flutter of her eyelashes or sensual curve of her lips and she would've been handcuffed and on her knees in ten seconds flat.

Instead, she quit.

His ego didn't appreciate the brush-offs. Claire was the only woman who had ever told him no. Rather, she had never given him the opportunity to expand the parameters of their relationship. He respected her boundaries. He respected her.

He wondered if she responded to him now because she believed him to be a stranger or if some part of her recognized who he really was—and that she could trust him. He hoped that was case, especially since he was putting more than just trust on the line tonight. He was betting his heart.

For a long moment, he stared at the crown of her head. The rasp of her rapid breathing infiltrated his jumbled thoughts. Should he continue? Or should he admit who he was?

If he told her now, he would break her trust forever. Whoever had tried to dominate her before had not given her control of the situation. He needed to know more about that relationship and how it had affected Claire.

One night wasn't going to be enough.

He wanted much, much longer with his beautiful Claire. He wanted . . . forever.

His heart raced as both love and lust wound through him. He would give her what she craved. He only hoped she would still want him after he took off the mask.

"I want you on my table," he said, keeping his voice low and raspy. "I want you naked and writhing and begging."

He heard her excited inhalation of breath and noted her trembling shoulders. Anticipation and excitement raced through him.

"Stand up, Claire."

She wobbled to a standing position and kept her gaze on the floor. God, she was beautiful. His cock was hard and aching, pressing almost painfully against the zipper of his pants. He couldn't wait until she earned her reward . . . until they would both be worthy of exquisite pleasure.

Claire kept her gaze on the floor. She was so nervous she felt her stomach quiver with nausea. And yet submitting to her master had created a state of arousal that went beyond mere sexual stimulation. She had never enjoyed the way Phillip made her feel. She realized now that Phillip had tried to master her only to please himself. This man's demands created answering needs within her. She wanted to please him. She wanted to obey him. And in doing so, she found freedom.

"Undress," he commanded softly. "Slowly. And look at me."

Claire raised her head and looked directly at him. In the shadow-filled dungeon, her masked lover looked very much like the dark, tortured hero of a Gothic romance. She couldn't wait to see him naked, to feel his flesh slide against hers. Her breath hitched as she thought about the way his cock would feel with that first, sweet thrust. Her pussy clenched and the moisture of her desire rolled down her thighs.

Since she was wearing only the dress, taking it off would pretty much end the striptease. She had no music, only the tumultuous beat of her heart and the rasp of her rapid breathing. She languidly turned so that her back faced him. Her fingers drifted down her hips and eased the dress up so that the curve of her ass showed.

She waited a beat, then dropped the cloth. It fell softly against her calves. She heard the sharp intake of his breath and smiled.

"Will you unzip me, master?" she asked.

He yanked up her dress and smacked her buttock. The blow stung, but she managed to keep from crying out. He caressed the abused flesh with his fingertips.

"I didn't think I needed to teach you manners."

Claire's heart beat frantically. Her ass throbbed, but her body went hot. God, she wanted him more than any man she'd ever known. Even though her stomach roiled at the mere thought of taunting him, she whispered, "Maybe you do."

He drew flush against her, his arms draping her waist. His lips pressed against her ear. "Are you deliberately disobeying me, Belle?"

She said nothing. He nibbled her earlobe; then he chuckled. His hot breath cascaded down her neck. "You are, aren't you? Hmm. You're being a naughty girl. Do you know what I do to naughty girls?"

Sweat dotted her forehead. Her body trembled so badly, she thought her knees might give way. She figured his question was rhetorical, so she didn't answer.

She closed her eyes and licked her lips, praying he wouldn't stop holding her. She might slide to the floor if he removed his support. She felt utterly boneless; her body was liquid fire, reacting to his words, his touch.

He drew her arms behind her back. Cuffing her wrists with one hand, he pulled her backward. "Don't stumble, Belle. Not once. Or I'll extend your punishment."

He tugged her backward and she managed to keep up with him. Her high heels protested the awkward movements, but didn't betray her feet, thank God. She was reminded of that oft-quoted phrase about that famous dancing duo: *Ginger Rogers did everything Fred Astaire did, except backward and in high heels.*

The next thing she knew, she was standing in a darker part of the room. Her master let go of her hands. She heard a rattle of chains above her head, but she didn't look. Whatever she was in for, she'd didn't want to add to it by trying to see what he was doing.

He lifted one arm and clasped her wrist inside a fur-lined manacle; then he did the same to her other arm. The pose wasn't uncomfortable, but it did feel strange. She wondered how long she could stand like this . . . wondered how long he planned to keep her imprisoned.

"I want you to understand why you're getting punished," he said. His breath was ragged. Oh, God. He was going to enjoy whatever lovely torture he administered.

So was she.

He walked into another corner of the room. She could barely make out his shape as he bent down and rummaged in what she thought might be a trunk.

"First, you asked me for a favor and you didn't say please."

She heard him rattle objects. Was he doing that for her benefit? If he was hoping to add to her tension, he was doing a damn fine job. He must've thought she'd moved beyond hand spankings.

Her mouth went dry and her throat knotted. *Oh, hell. What have I done?*

"Second, you told me I needed to teach you manners—and that is *my* decision, Belle, not yours. Then you failed to call me Master."

He stood up, his back to her, and then he circled the room—probably so that she couldn't see which implements he'd chosen. Her heart hammered now and she was sweating everywhere; beads of moisture rolled between her breasts.

Her swollen pussy ached for relief. She didn't think it possible to get any wetter. Her nipples were pebbled against the soft fabric of her dress. With only his voice and his dark promises, he had managed to get her into a glorious state of titillation. She licked her dry lips as expectancy settled low and hot in her stomach.

"You didn't answer my direct questions," he continued. "That's four infractions so far."

So far? Oh! He was right behind her. She heard the soft scrape of his shirt being removed. Then his shoes thunked to the floor. When he came around to face her, she saw that he wore only his black pants and mask.

He was magnificent. He was muscled—oh heavens, was he! His washboard stomach begged for her fingers, for her mouth. A light sprinkling of dark hair covered his pectorals, leading down his six-pack abs to his pants.

"Finally, you deprived me of your striptease. I very much wanted to see you slide out of that dress. I wanted to see you reveal yourself to me inch by inch." He looked at her. "I'm disappointed, Belle."

Damn. She didn't want to disappoint him. She just wanted to up the ante. "I'm sorry, master."

His smile was whip thin. "I accept your apology, Belle. But I expect you to take all of your punishment."

"Yes, master."

"Do you remember what I told you about the safe words?"

"Yes, master. I must say 'yellow' if I feel things are getting too intense. I must say 'red' if I feel I'm in danger."

"Very good," he said. He smiled approvingly. "You turn me on, *ma fleur*. I like it when you're good. And I love it when you're bad."

She resisted the urge to grin. Instead, she tried to look penitent, but she suspected he saw the humor flash in her eyes.

He stepped closer and raised his hand. She saw something sharp and silver flash in his grip. Oh, my God!

"Yellow!" she cried.

Stunned, he looked at her; the scissors hovered above the vee of her dress. He immediately stepped away and dropped his arms.

"What's wrong?" he asked.

"N-no blades," she said. "Please."

"I don't use knives and I don't do blood play. It's dangerous, and quite frankly, I abhor the idea of cutting my subs."

Tears pricked her eyes. Shit. She didn't want to end the game, but he had reminded her of her last night with Phillip. That rat bastard had told her then she wasn't what he needed, that she was too afraid to make a good submissive. That she was worthless.

And she had told him to fuck off.

But deep inside, she had believed his words. She knew how to be a good employee. She knew how to be a decent human being. But when it came to expressing her own sexuality—to getting what she needed from a lover—she believed he'd been right. Phillip's ugly words echoed in her mind: *Maybe you're frigid, Claire. Did you ever think of that? God, you're pathetic.*

"Our game is suspended. I'll take you down."

"No," she said. "Please."

He studied her for a moment, probably trying to determine her mental and emotional capacity. That he even took a moment to consider her needs made him a hundred times better than Phillip. Her master deserved more from her than this display of cowardice.

He showed her the scissors. "I planned to cut off your dress. I only wanted access to your luscious body." He tossed the scissors away; they landed with a clunk somewhere on the floor behind him.

"Thank you, master," she managed.

To her disappointment, he reached up and released her from the cuffs. He rubbed her tingling wrists; then he massaged her arms. "Relax, *ma fleur.*"

He rubbed her shoulders, easing the tension knotted on either side of her neck. His gentleness was nearly her undoing.

Was their evening over? Had her fears driven him away? She looked at him. The mask barred his expression, but she was close enough to see the wariness in his gaze.

"Master, are you . . . done with me?"

Seven

. . . .

"**N**ot by a long shot," he reassured her. He stepped back. "Turn around."

She did as he asked. He unzipped her dress and pushed the material off her shoulders. It pooled at her feet. He kneeled behind her and helped her disentangle her heels from the cloth.

"Walk to the table, where the candles are lit."

It was on the opposite side of the dungeon. She walked to the table and stood next to it, her gaze on the floor as she waited for him to join her.

To her shock, he kneeled at her feet, his fingers stroking her belly and ribs. She realized then he was touching her scars. Three lines on her belly, each one about two inches long.

"Who did this?"

He sounded furious, but she knew his anger wasn't directed at her. She had told no one of her true relationship with Phillip. She had broken up with him three months before she'd gotten the promotion to executive assistant. Her thoughts drifted to Lucius. He was kind and laughed easily, but underneath that slick playboy exterior was a man who knew what he wanted and how to get it. She had liked him because he knew when to ask her . . . and when to command her.

She gasped. For the last two years, she had been in a Dominant/submissive relationship and hadn't even realized it. That was why she responded to Lucius the way she did; that was why she thought she was in love with him. She really was a damn coward. Instead of facing Lucius and telling him the truth about her feelings, she had run away.

A sob caught in her throat. God! What the hell was wrong with her? Phillip had taken what she'd fantasized about since she was a teenager and turned it into something dirty and wrong. Then she'd followed Lucius around like an obedient puppy, never admitting to herself, much less to him, that she wanted him more than her next breath. And now, here she was, giving in to her sexual wants, facing her fears, with the wrong man.

"Red."

Her master rose swiftly. "Are you all right?"

"I've made a terrible mistake." Tears rolled down her cheeks. "I'm sorry. I have to go."

"Are you leaving because I asked about the scars? Or because you don't want to be punished?"

"I can take the punishment," she said softly. "But I'm in love with someone else. It's wrong to be here with you, without at least telling him how I feel." She leaned forward and kissed his jaw. "Thank you."

Claire turned away, but he enchained her wrist. "Wait a minute."

She was feeling more and more foolish by the second. She was standing naked in high heels with a shirtless masked man. She didn't know what she wanted anymore. But at least she still knew *who* she wanted.

Lucius.

"I have a confession," he said. "But before I tell you my secret, will you please tell me about your scars? Who hurt you, Belle?"

What was the harm in telling him about Phillip? And she was curious about his confession. What could he possibly tell her that would merit the worry in his voice?

"Three years ago, I graduated from college with my journalism degree and managed to nab a low-level position with *Bad Boy Magazine*. That same year, I met Phillip Rose at the coffee shop in the building where I worked. He was an advertising exec for another magazine.

"Anyway, after Phillip and I had gone out for a while, I told him about some of my . . . fantasies. He said that he was a Dom and he had only been waiting for me to realize I was a submissive. But everything we did felt wrong. I kept trying because I wanted it to match how I felt when I fantasized about domination."

Claire shook her head and sighed. "One night, Phillip took me to a public dungeon. He collared me and dragged me around on a leash. Then he hooked up with another Dom and took me into a private room. Things didn't feel right to me, but I trusted Phillip. I thought I was being a good submissive. After tying me up, the other Dom held a knife over a candle flame, then applied it to my stomach.

"I screamed bloody murder and scared Phillip so badly, he made the guy stop. I told him I had to go to the ladies' room, so he untied me. Instead, I went home and packed all the stuff he kept at my apartment."

"What happened next?"

"Phillip showed up a couple hours later. He was furious to find his things outside the door and that I had already changed the locks. He said a lot of shitty things, calling me a frigid bitch among other insults. But I'd had enough. I figured that I wasn't a submissive, that I just liked thinking about it and not doing it."

"You are what you want to be," he said. "A good Dom always puts the needs of his sub above his own needs. A Dom and a sub are two halves that fit together. His pleasure is always derived from his sub's pleasure. It can be a wonderful journey to take with the right person."

"I know that now," admitted Claire.

"I'm glad." He looked at her. "I promised to tell you my secret if you shared your past with me."

Claire looked at him, her heart thumping. His hand went to the mask, and suddenly, she didn't want to know who wore it.

Then it was too late.

The cloth lifted away and she was looking into the eyes of Lucius Devereaux.

Claire stared at him, caught between the urge to throw herself into his arms and to punch him in the jaw.

"I should've known," she whispered. "It's always been this way with you. With us. God, I'm a fool."

She hurried out of his reach and found her dress. She'd barely picked it up when Lucius plucked it out of her hand.

"Tell me who you're in love with."

Anger churned in her guts. "The game is over." She grabbed for the dress, but he snatched it out of her reach. "Goddamn it!"

"Fine," he said. "I'll tell you who I'm in love with."

Claire snorted. "Yourself. Give me that dress!"

"I'm in love with you."

She quit trying to grab her clothes. Lucius must really want her if he was willing to say what he had never said to another woman. The "L" word dangled just out of reach of every female he'd ever dated. He never lied to them, but they often lied to themselves. She'd seen the starry-eyed beauties who couldn't accept his good-bye. They were devastated. She didn't want to end up like one his castoffs.

"Nobody can have you," she said, shucking off her shoes. She'd walk to her room buck-ass naked. In this hotel, nobody would bat an eyelash. "You don't love, Lucius. You possess. No . . . you *rent*. You don't want me—at least not forever."

"Don't tell me what I want." He used his Dom voice and she stopped in her tracks. "I love you, Claire. Why would I say that just so I could have sex with you? This isn't about sex!"

Claire looked at him. He was fucking serious. He *loved* her? She wouldn't have believed it possible. "Why did you buy me?"

"To save you." He tossed the dress to the farthest corner of the room. "Why did you allow yourself to be bought?"

She couldn't justify why she'd stayed on that stage. She could've left at any point—not even Lady Pink's vicious whip could've stopped her exit. Nobody had forced her to participate in the slave auction. Phillip might have been her first and admittedly worst foray into the BDSM world, but he hadn't driven away her urges—just like he hadn't satisfied them.

"I wanted someone to think I was worthwhile. I wanted to serve someone who would cherish me and honor me and give me what I crave." She looked at him, tears filling her eyes again. "I never thought it would be you."

"I love you." He stepped close to her and tilted her chin. "Tell me who you're in love with."

"You," she said, crying harder. "I'm in love with *you*."

"Good. Then you won't be opposed to marrying me."

She nodded. Happiness chased away her anger, her confusion, and her doubts. "But I'm still quitting my job."

"You can do anything you want," he said. "What we do in the privacy of our home is our business and ours alone. You are mine, and I am yours."

Lucius embraced her, holding her tightly as she wept. After a while, her tears dried, but he held her close, stroking her back and whispering sweet nothings.

"C'mon," he said. "I want to draw a bath for you. I'll wash your hair, too."

"What about my punishments?"

"We're starting over," he said. "Clean slate. No more secrets, Claire. And no more lies."

"Yes, master."

Lucius woke up, feeling discombobulated. Next to him on the nightstand, the digital clock blinked a few minutes after three a.m. The king-sized bed with its oversized pillows and soft sheets felt empty.

Claire.

Panic shot through him as he rolled onto his side and checked the other half of the bed. She was gone. Had she changed her mind? No. He was confident that she wasn't going to leave him. And she certainly wouldn't sneak away in the middle of the night.

Even so, he shoved off the covers and sat up. That was when he saw the note next to the clock. Written on hotel stationery, the neatly printed word brought him instant arousal:

Dungeon.

He smiled. Reassured by Claire's note, he took his time getting out of bed. How long had she been waiting for him? Was she checking out the floggers or caressing that spanking table?

It excited him to think she was already splayed on that table, her firm, round ass ready for the whip. He wanted to run from the first-story bedroom to the spiral staircase, but he paced himself. Waiting would titillate her . . . and him.

Earlier, after he washed every inch of Claire's gorgeous body and shampooed her lovely hair, he had dried her thoroughly with a big, fluffy towel. Then he'd carried her to the bed and tucked her in, ordering room service and feeding her every bite of her fruit snack.

He held her as she drifted to sleep. He loved the feel of her in his arms; she felt so right tucked next to him. For a long time, he believed that he would never find love. He found plenty of female submissives to dominate, but not one that he wanted to spend his life with . . . not until Claire.

Fantasyland

For the last couple years, they'd managed a complex and subtle dance of domination and submission, but now that she was truly his, he could explore the depths of their relationship. His heart squeezed. God, he loved her. The sensation was so new, so beautiful, he couldn't quite believe it was his to cherish.

He couldn't wait to begin her training.

And apparently, neither could she.

He climbed the stairs, anticipation thrumming through him.

Eight
. . . .

Claire lay flat against the spanking table. She wasn't sure how long she'd been in the dungeon, but she was prepared to wait all night.

Earlier, she had spent a few minutes examining some of the furniture and devices. On one wall were several floggers and whips. She touched them in awe. The leather straps felt soft against her fingertips—and she wondered how they would feel against her flesh.

Then she'd lit the candles, shut off the light, and crawled onto the table.

She didn't look in any drawers or in the mysterious trunk that Lucius had rummaged through earlier. She figured looking at what was within sight wouldn't break any rules, but opening what was closed might get her punished.

She shuddered in fearful delight.

The supple leather next to her skin felt wonderful. She could only cuff her ankles, but she knelt on the slat and flattened the rest of her body against the slanted table. She lay there, thinking about Lucius and all the yummy things he could do to her on this table.

"Claire."

Her pulse skittered. Oh, God. He was using his Dom voice—that sexy rasp that demanded everything from her. Her pussy clenched, already wet with anticipation.

"Hmm. You have a beautiful ass."

"Thank you, master."

She felt him tighten the cuffs around her ankles. Then he rounded the table and squatted in front of her. Lovingly, he manacled each of her wrists.

He leaned forward and brushed his knuckles against her temple. "Are you ready?"

"Yes, master."

He nodded; then he stood up. He was gloriously naked, his cock already at half-mast. He strode away, probably to decide which implement to apply to her bottom.

She pressed her cheek against the table and closed her eyes.

A couple minutes later, she felt the tickle of many tiny "fingers" coast across her buttocks.

"This is a deer flogger," he said, dragging the falls along her buttocks again. "It gives your flesh a nice thud, but it won't sting. It's for low-intensity sensation play."

The straps suddenly disappeared.

Wham! She felt the smack of the tails against the middle of her left buttock. She sucked in a startled breath. He smacked her right buttock. He snapped the flogger expertly on each buttock twice more.

Oh, God. It felt so good.

She bit her lower lip and pressed her aching pussy against the leather table.

The falls drifted across her ass and down her thighs. The light touches felt nearly as good as the sudden thuds.

Wham! Wham! The flogger landed on each of her thighs. Claire moaned, pressing harder against the table. Her nipples stiffened and her entire body tingled.

The flogger kissed her back, trailing her spine to tickle her shoulders. The tails wiggled down her skin again and the nearly unbearable sensations crawled over her flesh, making her even hotter.

Wham! He hit one buttock.

She tightened for the next hit, but it didn't come. Seconds ticked by. Just as she relaxed—*Wham!* Another thud hit her ass. Lucius didn't stop. He flogged her faster and harder until she lost her breath and her body quaked at the rapturous assault.

Claire moaned. Her hips pumped against the table, the leather wet from her primed pussy. Her body hummed with desire, with aching need.

Lucius flogged her ass again, using the same quick, hard

thuds, and she felt almost apart from herself, detaching into a place of pleasure so intense, she nearly drowned in it.

As she floated in this lovely space, Lucius fumbled with her ankle cuffs. She barely felt him rub her feet and calves. Her ass felt marvelously sore.

"Claire."

Her eyes flickered open. Lucius unbound her wrists, massaging them. He looked at her with such love, such longing, she felt herself return to Earth.

"Master."

"I know exactly what you need," he said. "What we both need."

He crawled onto the table with her and rolled her onto her back. He covered her, his hard cock sliding between her slick folds, and then he sucked a turgid peak into his warm mouth.

"Oh!" She arched against him, wrapping her legs around his waist and digging her fingernails into his shoulders. "Please!"

He suckled her other nipple. Tiny lightning strikes erupted from her breasts to her belly to her weeping cunt. Her hands scraped down his back to his buttocks.

"I love you, Claire," said Lucius. His gaze was on hers as he slid his cock inside her.

"I love you, too."

He thrust deeply, his eyes never leaving hers. His hands wrapped around her shoulders as he plunged his cock into her over and over.

"Lucius!" she screamed as her body plunged into heat and light and delicious bliss. Her orgasm surged over her, stealing her breath and her sight. She held on to him tightly, her nails digging into his ass as she rode the incredible wave.

"Yes, Claire! I'm coming!" He thrust hard and deep, his cock nearly impaling her womb as his seed spilled.

They held on to each other, trying to catch their breath and regain control of their wild heartbeats.

After what seemed like an eternity, Lucius rolled to his side and gathered her close.

Lucius kissed her. His lips were warm and pliant. He slipped his tongue inside to mate with hers and her body revved up for another round. When he let her up for air, she pressed her fingers against her swollen lips.

"Will it always be like this?" she asked.

"No." Lucius grinned broadly. "It will only get better."

Seduce Me

· ·

Isle of Romance

Although you will most certainly find fun, adventure, and romance at any of our island retreats, the Isle of Romance is all about the power and pleasure of seduction.

Every one of our properties on this beautiful island caters to the romantic. We will indulge your senses in every area—from exquisite dining experiences in our gourmet restaurants to superlative treatments in our spa facilities.

You will be pampered, adored, and satiated.

The Isle of Romance is perfect for honeymoons, anniversary celebrations, or couple-only vacations.

We also have many activities that cater to singles. If you're looking for companionship, we suggest making an appointment with Fantasy Dates. At Fantasy Dates, you choose from a variety of packages designed to suit your needs. Then you choose your escort, based on a number of factors including looks, personality traits, and needs. The date with your ideal companion can go as far as you wish.

Remember, at Fantasyland, your pleasure is our business.

One
. . . .

Glenna Rosemont accepted the glass of champagne. Nerves tightened her belly and made her palms sweat. *This is stupid. This is so utterly stupid.*

Standing in a lushly decorated room crowded with women and men who all wanted a Fantasy Date did not make her feel better. Why should verification that the world was a lonely place give her the warm fuzzies?

She sipped the champagne and pretended to look at the paintings—all Impressionists—so that she wouldn't have to make eye contact with anyone else.

This little trip to the Isle of Romance in general and Fantasy Date in particular was courtesy of her mother. Lenora Rosemont was nothing if not persistent in the pursuit of finding the right man for her only daughter.

"How does shipping me off to Fantasyland to enjoy a pseudorelationship help with my love life?" she'd asked her mother in a last-ditch effort to avoid this trip.

"The only horse you've ever ridden threw you and stomped you flat." Mother handed her the brochure. "It's time to go riding again, darling."

The "horse" Mother referred to was Dr. Charles Moore. Nearly a year ago, he had ended their engagement mere weeks before their wedding.

Why? Because he married a stripper named Crystal in Las Vegas.

It was a blow to Glenna's heart and to her ego.

Charles had been the first man who'd ever looked at her as a person instead of a china doll. He had intelligence, warmth, and kindness. He had his own money, so he didn't need hers.

He'd been her first and only lover. He was gentle and sweet. Though she spent a great deal of time imagining their lives together, planning the wedding was left to her mother and the professionals. Glenna hadn't cared about the details surrounding the Big Day. She just wanted to be Mrs. Charles Moore.

Her family was not demonstrative. Expressing opinions on relevant topics was expected; showing emotion was not. The only place Charles ever showed affection was in their bedroom. Glenna swallowed the knot in her throat. Charles and she had been compatible. But they had not been in love.

It had been a bitter pill to swallow.

Fantasyland

Who needs a man? I have books! She supposed she had Charles to thank for Between the Pages. If he had not abandoned her, she wouldn't have spent all the time, energy, and money creating the cozy independent bookstore.

Glenna loved the little store, with its first editions and rare finds. Oh, she sold bestsellers, too, but she had no interest in the fluff written these days. Give her Charlotte Brontë or Shakespeare or Voltaire.

"Ms. Rosemont." The blond hostess—Tiffany or Bethany or some name ending with –any—appeared next to her. "Would you come this way, please?"

Glenna followed the woman through a door, down a hallway, and into another room. On one side was a floor-to-ceiling mirror—the biggest she'd ever seen. And she lived in a mansion with her mother, who obsessed about every line and wrinkle and thus had mirrors everywhere to indulge her beauty worries. And yet she wanted to be a grandmother. Go figure.

A white leather couch was placed in front of the mirror. The glass coffee table held a single thick binder. At the far end was a typical office: desk, chair, file cabinets.

"Your consultant is Joanne. She'll be with you in a moment. May I get you anything else, Ms. Rosemont?"

"No, thank you."

The blonde smiled and left, shutting the door behind her. Glenna stared at her reflection in the outrageously large mirror. Then she looked down at the binder.

She sucked down the champagne in one swig and wished

like hell she'd asked the hostess for another glass or two. Why had she caved into her mother's demands?

Glenna had allowed herself to be poked and prodded into this trip because she *was* lonely. She wanted a relationship. She wanted marriage and children. However, in order to find a man worth loving, she had to . . . to . . . *date*. And she would rather burn all her first editions than suffer through the archaic and confusing rituals involved with dating.

The door opened. A short brunette dressed in a black pantsuit and sensible black heels strode to the couch and sat next to Glenna. She offered a hand and said, "Hello, I'm Joanne."

"Glenna."

They shook hands. Joanne's gaze was frank. She wore little makeup and her hair was cut in a pageboy style. She looked like a no-nonsense professional, and for some odd reason, that made Glenna feel better.

"We have all your paperwork, Glenna. We've made several choices based on the answers to your questionnaires. Would you like to see your potential companions?"

"You might as well show me what Mother picked out." Glenna glanced at the binder.

"Ah. While your mother did request the opportunity to review your choices, only our clients are allowed to look at and pick from our companion roster."

Glenna smiled. "So you told her no? I'm sure that went over well."

Amusement flashed in Joanne's brown eyes. "I assure you, Glenna, that your Fantasy Date will be all that *you* desire. Are you ready?"

"Yes." *No. Hell, no. Get me out of here, please.*

Joanne opened the binder, and from the side pocket, she took out a credit card–thin remote control. She pointed it at the mirror, which turned gray then clear.

"Go on," said Joanne. "Have a look."

Her heart pounding, Glenna stood up and walked to the glass. "Can they see me?"

"No. Give me your top three choices. Then we'll look at their profiles, and you can pick the best one."

Glenna felt like a kid with her nose pressed against a candy store's window. At least a dozen men lounged around a large room. Most were shirtless. Some wore jeans and others shorts and still others boxers. A large-screen television blared CNN. Some sprawled on a couch and watched it. Two men were working out: One ran on a treadmill and the other lifted weights.

They were all hot. GQ models trapped behind glass. Muscled chests, chiseled profiles, narrow hips, long legs . . . dear God, a smorgasbord of maleness that overwhelmed and titillated Glenna.

Joanne had not gotten up. The consultant sat on the couch and waited patiently for her to make a decision. Three decisions.

Glenna walked from one end of the mirror to the other.

She paused, turning to look over her shoulder. "They all match my . . . uh . . . expectations?"

Joanne nodded. "Not everyone is a perfect fit, but the ones you're looking at now are the closest to your requirements."

Glenna returned to the mirror. She felt guilty, like Arthur Dent in *The Restaurant at the End of the Universe* when the cow came out and asked him to choose his steak. Here she was viewing specimens and being asked to choose her steak.

Well, here goes.

"The guy on the treadmill." She looked over the four men lounging on the furniture in front of the television. She rarely watched TV, preferring books over mindless distractions. She wanted someone with an attention span, so she skipped over those watching the big screen.

The guy lifting weights was too bulky. He reminded her of the Hulk. She spied one man leaning against the wall looking at a magazine. Hmm. Well, he was the only one reading anything, so he won a spot by default. She pointed at him and said, "The blond in the faded jeans reading *People*."

"Pick out one more," said Joanne.

Glenna looked over the men again. She spotted a redhead standing near the closed door. His spiked hair was wet, and he wore only a towel around his waist. He leaned next to the doorjamb with his arms crossed, looking really pissed off.

She watched him, curious. He didn't appear to fit in with the rest of the men. Not that she could tell much about any of them through three inches of glass. Then he looked up, seemingly straight at her. He had eyes as green as pond moss. Her heart skipped a beat, then restarted at a wild pace.

"Him," she said, her voice cracking. She cleared her throat. "I want the redhead in the towel."

"Who?" Joanne rose from the couch and joined Glenna at the window. She brought the binder with her and thumbed through it. "I don't have his picture or profile."

"Never mind about the other two," said Glenna. "He's the one I want."

Joanne smiled. "Let me track down his information and then we'll discuss your package options."

Glenna nodded. Joanne went to the office area and picked up the phone. While her consultant made inquiries about the mystery man, Glenna took the opportunity to study the redhead. He was probably six feet tall and well-muscled. His chest had a light dusting of red curls. His nose had an endearing crook in the middle, and there was an intriguing scar that ran along his left cheekbone.

He was the imperfect one among the perfect. And she wanted him.

"Are you sure you don't want to consider other companions?" asked Joanne as she crossed the room.

"No," said Glenna. "He's the one."

"Okay." Joanne glanced at the window, then at Glenna. Her smiled was a little too fixed to be real. "Have a seat. I'll return in a few moments."

She retrieved the remote and pointed it at the glass. It turned into a mirror again.

After Joanne left, Glenna stared at her own reflection again. She'd inherited her looks from a family with good genes—just like she'd inherited her money from a family whose wealth was generational. She was careless about her beauty, much to her mother's distress, and grateful for the money, which allowed her to indulge in her true love: book collecting.

She looked herself over. She wore her blond hair long and straight with bangs. Her eyes were light blue, often compared to a glacier. Then again, so was her attitude. She had Lenora's heart-shaped face, but not her collagen-plump lips. Because she refused beauty treatments and plastic surgery, her lips were on the thin side. But she had great cheekbones and skin as pale as moonlight.

Because of her looks and her money, she had been wooed numerous times by men in her social circles. If even one man had courted her because she was interesting or sexy or funny, she might've attempted dating. However, the motive had always been the same: She was a good match. She was, in their eyes, the perfect accessory for a busy man collecting all the things needed for success. She was merely something to be checked off a list.

So she had refused to go to another party, dinner, or soiree. She'd boycotted dating, too. Then she'd taken a large chunk of her money and opened Between the Pages. She hired a full-time book restorer, a full-time employee, and a part-time shop assistant. She often went on trips looking for antiquarian tomes.

Her life, once she'd taken control, was wonderful. Except that she was lonely. She wanted to be loved. She wanted to be . . . wanted.

Sighing, she glanced at the mirror. Was she really hoping that Mystery Man could show her the way to her own heart? Would his ability to woo her for a day or two crack open her icy exterior?

There was only one way to find out.

Two
·······

"**N**o." Sean O'Malley strode past Joanne and into the locker room. "My asshole friends locked me in that bloody room with those pretty boys. I'm not for sale."

"Neither are they," said Joanne in a patient voice. She followed him. "They offer companionship to women who need a little romance in their lives."

"And they get paid for it." Sean grimaced. "What do you call someone who gets paid to have sex?"

"Lucky. Oh, come on! They draw a salary same as you," said Joanne. "Only you get to boss people around and threaten them with violence."

"I'm a Safety Agent." He grabbed the edge of his towel and looked at Joanne with brows raised. "You really want to see the show, love?"

"If I didn't know what an ass you·are, that Irish accent

would melt me into a puddle of goo." Joanne sighed. "Out of all those prime specimens, she picked you. You've substituted for me before."

"Once. And you'll remember I said never again."

Joanne threw her hands up in the air. "Okay, okay. I'll tell the client you're unavailable, and she'll have to settle for someone else."

Sean hesitated. "You're not putting me on, are you? She really wanted me? Just me?"

"Just you." Joanne looked him over, then shook her head. "I shouldn't tell you this because God knows your ego is big enough. She took longer than most of my clients to look over her choices. And she didn't have a visceral reaction to anyone—except you."

The last time Sean had substituted as a companion, the whole experience had been miserable. It wasn't that the woman hadn't been beautiful or charming. Hell, she'd made it damned clear she'd go to bed with him. No, he hadn't liked the feel of being someone's arm candy. She'd paraded him around like a damn trained monkey. He put up with rude pats on his ass and smarmy comments. And at the end of the evening, when she grabbed his crotch and told him it was time to play cowboy, he'd told her no.

He didn't know how the other men put up with that kind of crap.

"Fine," said Sean, knowing he was going to regret agreeing to this nonsense. "But if we don't hit off, I walk."

"Deal."

Fantasyland

* * *

For your first meeting with your Fantasy Date, what would you enjoy most:

     A. Walk on the beach
     B. Intimate dinner for two
     C. Dance at a nightclub
     D. Other

For "Other," Glenna had written: *Meet for tea and scones at a bookstore café.*

Now she sat at a tiny table in the café portion of a bookstore called Romancin' the Book. It was within walking distance of her hotel, tucked in between a store that sold bathing suits and beach accessories and a gourmet-gifts shop.

She sipped her green tea sweetened with honey and waited for the luscious Sean O'Malley.

She had tried to dress casual, which for her meant white chinos, a pink striped top, and diamond stud earrings. To show off her pedicure, she'd chosen her jeweled T-strap Manolo Blahnik high heels. She'd pulled her hair into a ponytail and fluffed her bangs.

Nervously, she sipped her green tea. What if he didn't show? What if he didn't want her? What if he— Oh, shit. There he was. Walking toward her. He was dressed in pleated black pants and a green dress shirt. The shirt complemented his fabulous eyes.

She tried not to drool.

Social graces were second nature. She rose, smiled brightly, and extended her hand. "Hello, I'm Glenna."

He took her hand and shook it heartily. "Sean."

Wow. He had quite the grip. She half expected him to press his lips against her knuckles and say something romantic.

Instead, he plopped into the chair across from hers and looked her over. "You're pretty."

This announcement was made grudgingly.

"Thank you." She resumed her seat, at a loss. She pushed the plate of scones toward him. "Would you like to try one?"

"Not particularly." He looked around the bookstore and grimaced. "You like books, I guess."

"Yes."

Their first meeting was not turning out well at all. He was so handsome—the kind of handsome she wanted to nibble and lick. And that sexy lilt to his words . . . yummy. If only she could give in to the lust. Say something outrageous like "Take me into the alley and fuck me."

Her cheeks heated, and she looked at the cardboard cup that held her cooling tea. She could never make that sort of demand. Never say—much less *do*—something that naughty.

"What do you do, Sean?" She smiled. "When you're not a Fantasy Date, I mean."

"This and that." His gaze landed on her, dipped to her mouth, and then bounced away. "What do you do?"

I'm a matador. I'm a deep-sea diver. I'm a stripper. She sighed. "I own a bookstore."

"If you dislike it so much, why don't you sell it?"

Glenna looked at him, surprised. He had misinterpreted her reaction. So much for instant kinship. "I love my shop. Books are my passion."

"Oh." His gaze skimmed her mouth again. Her heart stuttered. Did he want her? But no, his eyes conveyed intense boredom. His arms were crossed, a clear sign of close-mindedness. Obviously, he didn't want to be there.

"What are your other passions?" he asked.

Like you care. "I have none." She stood up, suddenly furious with him, with herself, with the whole situation. "I'm sorry I wasted your time. Good evening, Sean."

She hitched her purse over her shoulder and strode away.

Sean watched Glenna hurry through the cooking section and bolt out the door. *Great job, Sean.* He sighed and considered his options. His thoughts drifted back to Glenna.

She was pretty—the real kind of pretty. On Fantasyland, there were a lot of gorgeous women, many who'd bought their beauty and paid a price every day to keep it. But not *her.* And that gave her some points.

She's not a cricket match, you idiot.

Sean looked at the scones. She had bitten into one. Probably nervously. And he'd acted like an asshole. The minute he'd told Joanne yes, he regretted it. He spent most of the day stewing in resentment, thinking about how he didn't want to play silly games with a woman paying for the privilege.

He was a Safety Agent, damn it, not Don Juan.

But he wasn't an SA tonight. He sighed. The hurt in Glenna's eyes had been real. For whatever reason, she'd signed up for a Fantasy Date. He wasn't too fond of the program. He didn't like the fakery of it all. But whatever her reasons for being there, she'd picked the one man who wasn't on payroll as a lothario.

He found that interesting. And he found her attractive. She was so proper, so perfect. An ice princess he very much wanted to melt.

Bloody hell.

Even though it was already dark, the boardwalk was crowded with people hitting the shops, restaurants, and dance clubs. Glenna wound through the happy tourists, horrified at the threatening tears. For God's sake! Nothing had happened to warrant crying. Had loneliness and sexual frustration turned her into a simpering fool?

Going against the tide of people who were enjoying their time on the Isle of Romance was like trying to swim upstream. The beach was mere steps from the boardwalk, so she cut across and found herself sinking into the soft sand.

Wonderful.

She toed off the heels, then scooped them up by the straps. The lights strung along the boardwalk kept the beach well lit. Several couples, most of them holding hands, wandered close to the shoreline. The ocean was black velvet; its gentle waves whooshed against the shore.

Glenna didn't feel like she belonged here. Not on the beach. Not on this island. And certainly not as a Fantasy Date. For a moment, she stared at the ocean. How nice it would be to stand near the waves and have the water tickle her feet.

Sighing, Glenna turned and walked down the beach toward her hotel. She would order room service and read *Jane Eyre*. Tomorrow, she would book the first trip she could off the island.

As she neared a flight of wooden steps that would take her onto a less-crowded spot on the boardwalk, she heard an Irish-tinged voice say, "I'm sorry."

Glenna stopped and looked over her shoulder. Sean stood behind her, looking uncomfortable and contrite. How long had he been following her?

She turned to face him. "There is no reason to apologize. We simply didn't connect."

"It's hard to connect to a rude bastard." He stepped closer and tugged the high heels out of her hand. "Let's take a walk."

Glenna hesitated. Earlier, she had worked up the nerve to indulge her romantic fantasies with Sean. But now she was unprepared for him. She wasn't sure she could separate fantasy from reality. No, it was worse than that. She wanted the real thing with a person who had not been paid to enjoy her company.

"I accept your apology, Sean. You don't have to prove anything else to me." She held out her hand for the shoes. "I'll make sure you get full payment for your services."

"God." He dropped the heels into the sand and looped his fingers around her wrist, pulling her close. "You know how hard you make me when you talk all prissy like that?"

"H-hard?"

"Yes, love," he murmured. "Hard. You wanna feel how much?"

Glenna couldn't respond. Her face heated and she ducked her head. No reason for him to believe she was easily swayed by his crude words. Still, her pulse jumped and her body tingled.

"Am I embarrassing you?" he asked softly.

"Of course not. I very much appreciate your efforts."

He chuckled. "Glenna, you're too polite. Too beautiful. Too irresistible."

Glenna's mouth dropped open. He cupped her face and brushed his lips across hers. Her purse slipped from her shoulder and thunked to the sand.

His kisses were soft, unhurried. Flames licked through her with every meeting, every parting. She pressed her palms flat against his chest and tried to keep upright as he tenderly assaulted her mouth.

Lust. She thought she knew the emotion—but no, she had never felt this kind of raw, rip-your-clothes-off anxiousness.

He angled his mouth to better fit hers, and then . . . oh, then he dropped all pretense of gentleness.

His lips demanded sacrifice. His tongue plundered mercilessly. She moaned and he captured the sound. His mouth took hers again, and again until she felt conquered.

His hands dropped to her waist, then slid over her buttocks, holding her closer still. The ridge of his cock so intimately pressed against her womanhood sent electric thrills racing through her.

When he finally released her mouth, she clung to him as though he were a life raft in a turbulent sea. She stared at him.

"Why on Earth did you kiss me?"

"It's my apology." He frowned. "No, that's a lie. You looked so prim sitting in that café. You talk like a politician's wife." He met her gaze. "I want to see you messy. I want to see you speechless. But mostly, Glenna, I want to see you naked."

Three
· · · · · · · · ·

Sean waited for the princess to react. Would she slap his face? Give him a sultry invite to her room? Or faint in his arms?

What are you doin', boyo? Glenna Rosemont was too far out of his league. He shouldn't have followed her from the café. He felt guilty for being an ass. He figured he owed her an apology. She hadn't deserved his rancor. He'd agreed to the damn date.

And the kiss? Hell, he just wanted to rile her. To see if that icy politeness would melt. Oh, she had melted all right. Even now she trembled in his arms, looking at him as she considered his rather bold proposition.

"The Isle of Romance is about wooing, isn't it?" She slid out of his embrace and reached down to get her purse. "Women want romance."

"'And what's romance? Usually, a nice little tale where you have everything as you like it, where rain never wets your jacket and gnats never bite your nose, and it's always daisy time.'" Sean smiled at her shocked expression. "You know who said that?"

She considered him with so serious an expression, he had to look away to keep from kissing her again. Why did her prim and proper manner drive him into instant lust?

Finally, she asked, "Do *you* know who said it?"

"D. H. Lawrence." He wrapped his arms around her, pleased when she didn't try to scoot away. "Is that what you want? Pretty, polite, and pedantic?" He dragged his lips over her jaw. She smelled so good. And her skin was soft as silk. "Or do you want real and messy and wild?"

"Oh, my." She tilted her neck so that he could have better access. He licked the lobe of her ear and whispered, "Let's go to your room, Glenna."

"'A life spent making mistakes is not only more honorable but more useful than a life spent in doing nothing.'" She looked at him, and he saw the doubt in her gaze. But hovering there was the desire to be spontaneous, to risk. "George Bernard Shaw."

"I always did like ol' George." Sean grinned. "Let's go make some mistakes."

Glenna stood in the luxurious bedroom of her hotel suite, tugging on her diamond-clustered earlobe. Now that she was standing close to the bed with her delectable Fantasy Date watching her, she wondered about risk versus regret. She was quite sure that sleeping with this man who made her heart race and her mind fog would be a very big mistake.

Sean leaned against the doorjamb, her Manolo Blahniks dangling from his right hand.

"I like you in diamonds," he said. "So keep in the earrings and wear these." He lifted up the high heels. "Everything else goes."

Glenna pressed a hand against her neck. "W-what about you?"

"Don't worry, darlin'. By the end of the night, we'll both be naked and sweaty." He sauntered to her and placed the heels on the four-poster bed behind her. He tugged the band out of her hair. Blond curls cascaded to her shoulders. His lips grazed the shell of her ear as he whispered, "Take your clothes off."

His demand was threaded with lust. Nervous didn't begin to describe her state of being. She was terrified. How had a night of romance turned into a night of wild sex?

Sean stepped back, crossed his arms, and stared at her. His lips hitched. In his eyes, she saw his disbelief. He didn't think she'd take off her clothes. What was he doing? Waiting for her to throw him out?

Oh, she wouldn't fold so easily.

She took off her shirt, revealing her lacy white bra. His gaze dipped to her breasts and roamed across her cleavage.

Swallowing the knot in her throat, Glenna unsnapped her pants and pushed them down to her ankles. Her thong matched her bra.

Sean's gaze roved over her from blond locks to pedicure. When his gaze finally met hers, he looked as if he wanted to devour her.

Her stomach squeezed. She knew that he would leave if she asked. In fact, she suspected he thought she would chicken out. He'd been right about life being messy. It was never what you expected. If life was predictable, it was boring. Just like her life, which had become all about routines and staying in her comfort zone.

She reached back and unhooked her bra, cupping the front so that it wouldn't fall away. Sean watched her with greedy eyes. If she didn't know better, she'd think he'd forgotten about intimidating her.

Slowly, she worked one arm out of the strap—then the other. She stared right at him as she held the bra in place. He shifted his weight, as if he might pounce on her. His eyes were glued to her chest. For the first time in her life, she realized she had sexual power. She could tease Sean just as much as he teased her. She could make him wait, make him want.

"Take it off," he said, his rough voice edged with desire. "Now."

"What will you give me?"

"Give you?" His gaze flicked to hers. His grin was feral. "What do you want?"

Glenna hadn't thought about the answer to her own question. She was still amazed she had managed to be flirtatious. "Your shirt."

He said nothing. He merely unbuttoned the dress shirt and tossed it to the floor. She looked at his muscles, at the red curls on his chest.

She dropped the bra.

He fisted his hands as if to keep himself from touching her.

Her panties offered the only protection. It seemed silly to think of the thong as the last defense against Sean's lust. All the same, she sat down and put on the high heels.

Sean strode to the bed and knelt before her. She sat there, unsure what he would do. She was basically naked with a half-dressed god at her feet.

Sean's fingers drifted across her ankle and up her calf. The light touch sent shivers through her.

He was in no hurry, thank God.

His fingers tickled the underside of her knee and he leaned forward to press his lips on the top of her thigh. His right hand rubbed her other leg, inching toward her panties.

Her whole body tensed. She'd never felt such a mixture of lust and terror. She was treading unknown ground. Lovemaking with Charles had never been fraught with this kind of nerve-racking disquiet. She felt utterly vulnerable.

His forefinger slipped under the lace perimeter. "You're

wet." He looked up at her. His green eyes sparkled like emeralds. "I bet you're tight, too."

He was so *raw*. He didn't hide his feelings behind pretty words or gentle gestures. Heat swept up her body, a mixture of embarrassment and carnality.

"Stand up."

She did as he bade, though her legs threatened to buckle.

"Show me your pussy."

Uncertainty sliced through her. He looked at her, waiting for her to show courage or cowardice. He apparently didn't feel it necessary to offer encouragement or even additional demands.

The decision was hers.

Glenna slid off the panties and revealed that she was a true blonde. She'd gotten a bikini wax before the trip, and Sean seemed to appreciate the trimmed look of her pussy.

Sean moved close to her. Her breasts scraped his chest and her sensitive nipples hardened. She thought, given his predilection for cutting to the chase, he would simply push her to the bed and feast on her.

Instead, he gathered her into his arms and pushed back the loose tendrils of her blond hair.

"Darlin' Glenna," he murmured.

Oh so slowly, he brushed his lips across hers.

She shuddered with the pleasure. His moan feathered her mouth, and she breathed in the mint of his mouthwash.

Angling his mouth over hers, he tasted her again. His lips were like a butterfly dancing from flower to flower: He never stayed in one place, and each touch was light, quick.

He was seducing her with just his kisses. Showing her how much he wanted her. She understood the message. Her breathing was erratic, her eyes dazed, and her arms limp around his neck. Cupping her ass, he brought her close, pressing his jean-clad cock into the vee of her thighs.

Her heart pounded frantically; her body was awash in sensations that were both foreign and exhilarating. With his tongue, he traced the seam of her lips, then broke through the slight resistance and dipped inside for a real taste.

Her tongue shyly met his, and he held her tighter. Her palms pressed flat against his chest, and she felt the erratic beat of his heart. It thrilled her to know he was as turned on as she was.

Finally, he broke the kiss, pulling away just enough to look into her eyes. "How far do you want this to go?"

"How *far*?" She stared at him, astonished. "I'm naked. I'm in your embrace. And you just kissed me like I was the last chocolate truffle in the glass case. I believe I've made my position on this matter clear."

"Good." He released her and moved back. His eyes twinkled with wicked intent. "You're in charge, darlin'. What do you want to do?"

Four

G lenna considered her options. What she really wanted to do was to shock the hell out of him. She couldn't change her personality or her manners or the way she'd been raised. But Sean was giving her an opportunity to behave however she wished, without judgment or expectation.

It seemed silly to keep thinking about Charles, but he had been her only lover. Though he always worked to bring her to orgasm, she'd felt that their lovemaking lacked *something*. They had been two bodies working together toward mutual pleasure in a very staid, proper way. And that was not the same as spontaneous, passionate sex.

She looked at Sean from beneath her lashes. So he liked her prim words? Hmm.

She walked toward him, trying to hide her anxiousness behind a wide smile. She trailed her fingers up his chest, then looked up into his handsome face.

"I would very much like to . . ." She trailed off, nibbling her lower lip. She glanced away, pretending shyness. Then she gazed at him again. His eyes had gone dark, his body rigid. It startled her to believe she really did have the ability to make him want her. "Oh, my. I'm not sure if I can say . . . *that*."

"Try." The word was almost growled. Instead of frightening her, the roughness of his voice betrayed his own need. For her.

"I want . . . to . . . suck your cock."

"Jaysus." The Irish was thick. "I can't believe you said such a naughty thing with that prissy mouth."

"My prissy mouth is capable of much more." She reached down and unbuttoned his pants, then slid down the zipper. She tugged on the waistband, but he brushed aside her efforts and pushed down his pants and boxers. His thick cock sprang free, and Glenna nearly swallowed her tongue.

He was huge. Much bigger than Charles. Nerves plucked at her stomach as she wrapped trembling fingers around his hard shaft.

"I want to taste you," she said. "Please."

Sean watched Glenna kneel, and he nearly lost it. He was doing his best to romance her, though it wasn't red roses and gourmet chocolates. He figured she'd had enough of pretty rituals. Maybe he was egotistical enough to believe that showing her a good time in bed was what she really needed.

His eyes almost crossed as she cupped his balls. She was tentative at first, as if she didn't quite know what to do with his genitals.

She figured it out. She drew one testicle into her warm mouth, released it, and pleasured the other. Oh, God. Her tongue whipped up his cock, and then she drew the tip of his penis into her mouth.

She practiced taking his full length over and over. Her eagerness outweighed her inexperience, and soon she managed a rhythm that included suction and movement.

His hands fisted against his thighs. She was wild now. Her nails dug into his ass. She took his cock again, her rhythm doubled, her tongue flicking fast and furious.

"Glenna!" He reached down and pushed her face away. His balls tightened, his cock pulsing with the need to ejaculate. He inhaled steadying breaths, trying to stall the orgasm.

After a long moment of thinking about cold showers and baseball statistics, he looked down at her. Her gaze was wide-eyed and her face flushed.

"Did I do something wrong?" she asked.

"Hell, no. You did something right."

Her gaze dropped to his cock. Precome pearled the tip. She leaned over and licked it off.

"You're going to make me come."

"Why is that a bad thing?"

"Did I say it was?" He stepped out of his boxers and pants, bending over to take off his socks and shoes. When he was naked, he straightened. "Now it's my turn."

"Y-your turn?"

Sean helped Glenna to her feet, then scooped her into his arms. She laughed breathlessly, obviously startled by his action. He strode to the big bed and lowered her on top of the thick coverlet.

Her blond curls fluttered outward, her pearlescent skin gleamed, and her perfect toes wiggled in the expensive shoes. She looked like a castaway floating in a red velvet ocean.

Sean crawled onto the bed and lay next to her.

Side by side, they looked at each other. Glenna had never been with a man like this. His gentle exploration was strange to her. He made her shiver and tremble, sigh and moan.

Sean's fingers drifted across her arm, down her side, to her hip. He stroked her buttock, cupping it and kneading it. Then his hand moved leisurely to her thigh.

Glenna wasn't sure what was expected, so she lay on the bed and simply enjoyed what he was doing to her. Then Sean rolled her onto her back and covered her, his hardening cock nestled against her pussy.

He kissed her shoulder, and the soft press of his lips made her shudder. He tasted her collarbone, moved up her neck, and peppered kisses along her jaw. His green eyes were glazed with desire, his breath harsh against her lips.

"I've never wanted anyone like I want you," she said, and it was the truth.

Sean stretched her arms above her head. Her back arched slightly, pushing her breasts into his chest. Her nipples pebbled against his warm flesh.

"Say it again, Glenna. Say you want me."

"I want you."

She felt his cock jerk against her clit and knew he wanted to take her right now.

The slow melding of their mouths made Glenna's breath hitch and her heart pound. His tongue slipped into her mouth and danced with hers. When he was done kissing her senseless, Sean nuzzled her neck, his lips causing erotic shivers wherever they touched.

With one hand, he cupped her breast. His strong, warm fingers squeezed her flesh. He pinched her nipple, and the bud tightened almost painfully. He gave the same treatment to her other breast. It felt so good, so terribly wonderful.

His tongue flicked the peak. Pleasure jolted through her and she moaned. He laved her nipples, suckling one while his hand tormented the other. Then he switched mouth and hand while his cock rubbed against her clit.

Glenna ran her hands down his body. His buttocks were round and firm and she grabbed hold, rubbing her aching pussy against his hard cock.

Her whole body was in flames and she felt ravenous. She

wanted to make the torture last . . . and yet make it end at the same time.

Sean kissed his way down her body. Then he scooted between her legs, pushing them apart to nuzzle the flesh on either side of her pussy.

His tongue parted her slick folds and flicked her clit, teasing the hard nub. Glenna felt struck by a bolt of lightning. Charles had never kissed her there. And he had not expected her to put her mouth on his cock, either.

How could she have thought what they had shared was making love? There had been no passion, no desperate need, no obsession to touch or to kiss. She felt all those things and more with Sean, who was a stranger.

She couldn't focus on what that meant—and surely it meant something—because Sean's tongue delved into her slit, sipping on the evidence of her desire. Then his mouth settled on her clit and he sucked it.

Glenna arched, her breath catching in her throat. Sean did this crazy thing with his tongue, sucking and flicking and driving her closer and closer to her peak.

The orgasm swelled, waves of pleasure threatening, then burst, sensation after sensation rolling over her. She moaned and bucked and came.

Glenna barely had time to recover from the incredible orgasm. Sean left the bed, plucking his wallet from his discarded pants and withdrawing a square package. She hadn't even thought about protection, even though she was on birth control.

Sean wasted no time putting on the condom. Then he returned to the bed and ravished her thoroughly. He nuzzled the space between her breasts, kissing the soft flesh thoroughly before encircling her areola. He tortured both of her breasts with small, sweet kisses and quick stabs of his tongue.

Her hands threaded through his soft, thick hair. She pressed him closer. The sensations he caused were intense. Already heat settled between her thighs; her pussy was revving up for another round.

"Sean," she begged. "Please."

"I love the sound of my name on your lips." His lips paid homage to her rib cage. He tasted her navel, circling the flesh around it. His breath heated her skin; his thorough exploration of her body left her quivering and needy.

Oh, hell. Was he going down there again? Glenna felt her body go liquid.

His tongue's sudden invasion of her pussy shocked her. Just like that. He thrust deep, tasting her, groaning so loud she felt the vibration all the way to her very core. Her body felt gloriously afire.

Sean made a return trip up her body, his lips and fingers touching her everywhere, until she felt consumed by his lust.

He slid his arms under her and cupped her shoulders. His cock slowly penetrated her, and she was grateful that he took his time. It had been a while since she'd had sex, and Sean was rather large. All the same, she loved the way he filled her, stretching her, nearly touching the entrance to her womb.

Sean's head dropped to her shoulder, and he took a shuddering breath. "Jaysus. You're tight, darlin'. And so wet."

"Sean," she whispered, drawing her legs around his waist, "fuck me."

"What a filthy mouth you have." He grinned, but she knew he was on the edge. He began to thrust inside her.

In no time at all, they were lost in each other, trying everything to bring more pleasure to their union. They fucked wildly, all growls and sweat and motion.

The rocking of their bodies singed her. Erotic tension coiled tightly as his cock pierced her over and over again.

Glenna's ability to think faded. All she wanted was the no-strings-attached bliss Sean offered her.

"Glenna, I'm going to come!"

His words plunged her over the edge into beauty and light.

Sean thrust deeply, stilling, his face tight as he came.

It was then that Glenna realized that she wanted Sean to offer her more than one night in paradise.

Five
· · · · · · · ·

When Glenna awoke, she heard the soft snores of Sean, who still slept beside her. They'd left one of the small lamps on, and she was glad because it gave her enough light to look at Sean.

She was surprised that he hadn't left yet. She wasn't sure what to expect. Sean was, after all, just a Fantasy Date. There was never meant to be any permanence between them, though she found herself wishing for more than just mind-blowing sex.

How selfish she was.

She hadn't thought about what Sean might want. How many women did he date? How many ended up in his bed? God, she was being so stupid. To Sean, she was just another client. He was very good in bed, though he'd failed to be romantic in the traditional sense. No dinner, no small talk, no flowers.

But really, she hadn't missed those things.

If she had Sean only for tonight, then why not make the best of it? Even if what they had right now wasn't real, he had at least given her one gift: She wanted to find love and passion with a man who would love and cherish her. And who liked her to talk dirty.

He lay on his back, with one arm across his chest, and the other thrown carelessly above his head. She rolled on her side and looked her fill.

Glenna scooted his arm to the bed. Then she leaned over him and kissed his naked chest. His skin was taut, all muscled curves and ridges. She feasted on his pectorals, peppering kisses on every centimeter of flesh. She laved his tiny brown nipples into hardness, then flicked her tongue across each nub.

"Hello, darlin'."

She got on top of him and licked the space between his pecs, tasting the faint musk of his skin. They both probably smelled like sweat and sex. It was an essence she liked.

As she explored his body with fingers and lips, his hands were restless on her back, her shoulders, her buttocks. Then Sean looped his hands under her arms and pulled her forward so his mouth could ravage her breasts.

Zings traveled from her nipples to her pussy as he tugged one peak, then the other, between his teeth and flicked his tongue rapidly against the taut peaks.

Fantasyland

An ache bloomed in her pussy.

She popped out of his embrace, and he scowled at her. Laughing, she scooted down and rubbed her slick pussy against his cock. It pulsed against her flesh, hardening.

Anticipation trilled through her.

It nearly killed Sean to let Glenna torment him. Maybe it was ego, but he felt she was just figuring out her sensuality. He was glad to be her guinea pig, but damn, he wanted to devour her all over again. Not being the aggressor was alien to him.

Even so, he stayed put, fisting his hands in the covers to stop himself from tumbling her on her back and plunging into her sweet pussy.

She kissed his chest, laving at his flat brown nipples before dipping down to his rib cage and then his stomach. He shuddered beneath her lips and fingertips.

He loved the feel of her, the smell of her, the way she smiled. She rose above him, an ice goddess, and rubbed her pussy along the ridge of his cock.

Oh, God.

Leaning forward, she offered her breasts for him to feast on, and he did, cupping and kneading them, pinching the hard nipples until she moaned.

"Help me," she said. "Please."

She got onto her knees, her pussy hovering over his cock. He held on to his shaft while she pushed down, her sweet cunt taking every inch of him.

Her first movements were tentative. Soon, though, her uncertainty gave way to confidence.

She moved faster, her breathing shaky as she found her rhythm. Her blue eyes were glazed with passion. She was beautiful.

Her pussy quaked around his pumping cock. She rode him, if not with skill, then with enthusiasm. He played with her breasts, tugging on her nipples. She gasped, her eyes going wide.

Her orgasm was so strong, it squeezed out his cock. Her pussy sucked at his flesh, her come drenching his balls.

"Get on your hands and knees, Glenna."

Dazed, she rolled off and did as he asked. He got behind her and worked his cock into her pussy. He held on to her hips, plunging hard and fast. She moaned, rearing back to meet his frantic thrusts.

It was damn idiotic to fuck her without a condom, but he couldn't stop himself. He wanted her too much.

He fucked her until he couldn't stand it. Then he pulled out, and stroked his shaft into a shattering orgasm. His come splattered against her ass and back.

When he was finally able to draw a breath, he saw that she was trembling. Damn it. Had he hurt her?

"Glenna?"

She rolled onto her back, which was stained with his come, and parted her legs.

She moaned, one of her hands tugging a nipple, while the other rubbed her pussy.

Sean sat back and watched her pleasure herself. She was so responsive, so sensitive. She was gorgeous like this, wanton and sexy. Uninhibited.

She plunged one finger inside her own cunt, then two. Her palm rubbed her clit, her fingers penetrated her cunt, and her fingers twisted her nipple.

"Mmm. Yes! Yes!" Her hips lifted from the bed as she came.

Sean watched as her pussy sucked at her fingers. Her taut legs trembled. Her nipples looked rock-hard. Her face was a mask of ecstasy.

Finally, she collapsed to the bed. It seemed like forever before she opened her eyes. Sean met her gaze. Her cheeks bloomed red, and he shook his head.

"There's nothing about sex you should be ashamed of," he said. "I'll watch you do that again, if you like."

She smiled.

And Sean felt as though he'd been punched in the gut.

Was he falling for her?

No. *No way.*

Sean took her mouth in a gentle caress, his breath skirting her lips. Only when Glenna's mouth was pliant, willing, did he deepen the kiss, thrusting his tongue inside to mate with hers.

Glenna's skin prickled, as if electrified. She was learning about her own body, what she liked, what she didn't. Exploring her sensuality with Sean was a gift. And learning about him, about how to please, how to torment—that was a gift, too.

His lips moved down her throat, lingering at the base. He trailed a path to her breasts, cupping them in his hands to bring them closer to his mouth. His warm lips closed over one nipple.

He suckled, licked, nipped.

She wriggled, moaned, sighed.

He turned his attention to her other nipple, giving it the same torturous attention.

"Sean . . ."

His hand coasted down her stomach and found the strip of blond curls. He gently pinched her clit, released the nub, and pinched again.

Oh, sweet merciful heaven.

Sean laved her nipples and slipped two fingers inside her pussy. She moved in rhythm with his strokes, building the pleasure until it was nearly unbearable.

"I want you to fuck me, Sean."

"God in heaven. You're goin' to kill me, talkin' like that."

His Irish accent was thick. Every word, every touch, every movement sent streams of need winding through her.

Sean moved on top of her, parted her thighs, and entered

her in one swift stroke. With one hand, he captured her wrists and raised her arms above her head. With the other hand, he steadied himself over her. His cock filled her.

Sean's green gaze captured hers. "What did you say about fucking you?"

"Hard. Fast. *Now*."

He pounded into her. Still he held her wrists, his thumbs pressing against the erratic pulse. She bucked against him, her clit throbbing. Sensation after sensation vibrated from her core.

Then Sean, damn him, stopped.

"What the hell!" She grabbed his buttocks and thrust her hips.

"Now, now, darlin'. Patience is a virture."

"Screw patience!"

He chuckled as he got on his knees and opened her legs like a pair of human scissors.

Glenna, heart pounding and hormones raging, looked at him crossly. His grin promised wicked fun, so she wouldn't kill him. Yet.

He placed one of her legs between his, and put the other on his shoulder. Holding her ankle with one hand, he scooted closer and closer, sliding his cock inside her. The angle was odd, but it felt good.

"Put your hand on your pussy," he said. "I want to see you stroke yourself while I fuck you."

This *was* different. Raw. Exciting. Real.

Glenna moved her finger against her clit, sliding it through the wetness, caressing the sensitive nub.

Sean withdrew and entered, working his cock in and out of her pussy. As his pace increased, so did Glenna's pleasuring of her clit.

"I'm going to come," she moaned.

Sean's thrusts quickened. She heard his groans and gasps, felt the grip of his hand on her leg, and then she came, shattering against her own hand, her vagina pulsing around his cock.

"Glenna!" he shouted. He pulsed deeply within her.

He released her leg and left briefly to dispose of the condom. Then he returned and gathered her in his arms.

"You are amazing," he said, kissing her neck.

"So are you."

In the morning, Glenna awoke to find the bed empty. Last night, they had bathed each other, ordered room service, and watched television. It had felt too much like a real relationship. But no, Sean was a Fantasy Date. A paid companion. There was nothing real between them.

She sighed, feeling wonderful about her night of wild sex and sad about Sean. Honestly, she didn't even know him that well. He hadn't talked about himself, though he had asked her plenty of questions.

The last time they made love had been his good-bye. She felt it in his kiss, in his touch, in his slow taking of her.

She should've known that he would wait for her to fall asleep before he left.

As she rolled to her side and gazed at the spot where he'd slept, she saw the white rose and the folded note. Heart pounding, adrenaline pumping, she sat up and grabbed the lovely flower. The note was short:

You were my best mistake.
Sean

Glenna inhaled the sweet essence of the flower and smiled.

Six

. . . .

"What the hell is your problem, man?" asked Matt. "You've been an asshole all day. You need to get laid."

Sean resisted the urge to punch out his friend, since he was right. Sean had been an asshole all day—*because* he'd gotten laid.

She was wrong for me. I'm wrong for her. It was just sex. So what if I liked her? So what if I thought it might be nice to get to know her?

"Sean?"

"I don't want to talk about it."

"Whatever, man. I ain't your therapist."

They were walking along the dock, checking the status of guests who were preparing to leave the Isle of Romance. It was a routine perimeter check. Overall, Fantasyland was a safe environment, but tourists in any location attracted thieves and cons. There was no way to keep criminal elements out of Fantasyland entirely, which was why the resort employed so many SAs.

On the left side of the dock were the boats going to and from the Bahamas. Since it was Sunday, the dock was crowded with people headed to the airport. On the right side, was a beautiful ocean view and "photo opportunities."

Sean checked the right, and Matt checked the left. All was well.

"Let's do a beach check," said Matt. "Then it's lunchtime."

They parted at the end of the pier. Once again, Sean went right, and Matt went left.

Sean's thoughts returned to Glenna.

Damn it.

Glenna felt the cold slap of water against her feet. She dug her toes into the sand and looked across the blue water. Sometimes, looking at the ocean made her feel small. But today, she felt as though she were part of something bigger than she comprehended. A cog in the wheel of life.

She splashed into the water, walking until her toes barely touched the sand. She was determined to finish her vacation. Sean was a good lesson for her. He'd taught her about risk.

She was so busy thinking about the handsome Irishman

that she didn't prepare for the huge wave rolling toward her. It slammed into her, and she tumbled into the water. She couldn't figure out up from down. She tried to swim, but couldn't wrest herself from the swirling water.

Then she felt someone grab her arms and drag her toward light, toward air. She burst from the water and gulped in oxygen. Her rescuer held on to her waist as he swam toward the shore.

When they reached the beach, she coughed up water, spitting the salty liquid into the sand. Finally able to sit up, she found herself looking into the green eyes of Sean O'Malley.

"Are you all right, darlin'?"

She nodded. Her gaze dipped to his black T-shirt. On the right side of the shirt was stitched O'MALLEY and underneath some sort of symbol with an SA inside it. She'd seen that symbol in the paperwork she'd signed.

"You're not a Fantasy Date?"

Sean shook his head. "I'm a Safety Agent."

"Why were you in the room with all the others? As a joke?"

"The coworkers who locked me in there thought it was." Sean pushed her wet hair from her face, then plucked a piece of seaweed from it.

She pushed his hand away. "I don't understand."

"Joanne asked me for a favor. She said you picked me." He smiled. "I didn't want to disappoint you."

"Or you wanted to get laid."

"I won't deny it. What about you, Glenna? Did you get what you wanted?"

Her anger turned to ashes. How could she be mad at him? She'd paid outrageously for the privilege of dating the perfect man. Instead, she'd gotten the imperfect one. "I wanted romance and you gave me reality. You showed me passion. You made me want to fall in love."

Sean's gaze filled with tenderness. He took her hand and kissed her knuckles. "Stay."

"My bookstore—"

"I'm better than any book, darlin'." He dropped her hand and cupped her face. "Stay. *Please.*"

Glenna looked into his eyes and saw that he wanted her. Maybe for a while. Maybe forever. "Okay," she said. "Let's go make some mistakes."

Acknowledgments

I wish to thank my editor, Kara Cesare, because she keeps buying books and tells me I'm funny (in a good way) and doesn't kill me when I need extra time to finish novels.

I adore my agent, Stephanie Kip Rostan, who keeps selling books for me and tells me I'm funny (also in a good way) and doesn't kill me when I need her to ask Kara for extra time to finish novels.

I'm immensely grateful to the production team at NAL, who probably sees my name on the book schedule, groans collectively (on no, not HER), then does a fabulous job.

To my husband and our children: I love you. Now, leave me alone and let me write.

And to all those readers who buy my books: Thank you, thank you, thank you.